In Meadowlight

Also by Sussie Anie

To Fill a Yellow House

In Meadowlight

Sussie Anie

PHOENIX

First published in Great Britain in 2026 by Phoenix Books,
an imprint of The Orion Publishing Group Ltd
Carmelite House, 50 Victoria Embankment
London EC4Y 0DZ

An Hachette UK Company

The authorised representative in the EEA is Hachette Ireland,
8 Castlecourt Centre, Dublin 15, D15 XTP3, Ireland
(email: info@hbgi.ie)

1 3 5 7 9 10 8 6 4 2

A CIP catalogue record for this book is
available from the British Library.

ISBN (Hardback) 978 1 4746 2174 8
ISBN (Ebook) 978 1 4746 2177 9
ISBN (Audio) 978 1 4746 2178 6

Typeset by CC Book Production Limited
Printed and bound in Great Britain by Clays Ltd, Elcograf S.p.A.

FSC www.fsc.org MIX Paper | Supporting responsible forestry FSC® C104740

www.orionbooks.co.uk
www.phoenix-books.co.uk

PART ONE:

The House

First, nothing.

And then: a house.

Another house.

Another house.

A flat.

A house.

Another flat.

Another house.

And more.

And more.

And then, the house.

And from then: everything.

I

should anyone ask – these coming weeks – about the quiet

and

the space

and

whether any place in Meadowlight felt like

home

if they ask, she will say, sure, for a while, yes.

2

She had started to think of houses as numbers by that point. Each house has two numbers – minimum – in her mind. The first is the number of the house's position in the year; the second is the number that appears on the front door.

House eight (door twenty-nine): the house in which she bathed again. To wash there was an immersion; not a shower, but a deep soak. Under the foam, water roared around her ears. When she surfaced, she thought of baptisms.

House twenty-one (door ninety) brought a pet she tried to like: a mouse. She had never touched a mouse before and likely never will again.

And this, twenty-seven, will be the start. And so the end.

This house, twenty-seven, is also the first with its own name. The name – here, on a copper plaque by the front door – is Meadowlight.

'Temporary,' the client says, as they wait here, outside the house. It is their first time meeting in person. Mercy and the client. And the house. It is Mercy's first time seeing the house. The day is mild and sunshine teases between the clouds. The client is in a raincoat, by the door. Her hands are fussing with the keys. She stands with her head bowed, one boot on the step. She says she has been looking for a new name since she bought the place.

'It's nice,' Mercy says. 'A nice name for a house.'

Meadowlight.

She has the urge to say it, to hear it in her own voice. Instead she asks, 'So how long have you been living here?'

She'll come to that, the client says, as she turns the key in the lock.

'It's not easy to name a house,' she says. 'Though I should warn you, it's not a house.'

The client pushes the door, and steps into the hallway. The hallway runs the house's length, from front to back. It ends in the haze of the stained-glass window, where light glows in various hues from the garden.

'Come in,' the client says.

Inside the building, the air has an oaky musk. Underneath, it tastes of vanilla and smoke. The lighting is soft. No windows split the shade of the hallway other than the panels above the door and the stained glass at the far end. Instead, from the walls, paintings hang.

The client tells Mercy to remove her shoes, please, and leave her coat here. Her umbrella, too; everything in the cloak corner here, she says.

The wind pushes the door shut behind them. Mercy looks up to the glass panels above it, where daylight is spilling in. It is hard to name this feeling, of arrival, but also of return, a sense of standing again on a familiar frontier.

'All right,' the client says. 'Let's introduce you to the cats.'

3

It is a week post-interview, after that first visit to the house, and by now the client is far away, flying over the Atlantic. They will speak soon – tonight, she said, in an email this morning. Mercy read this message on her phone, on the train up from London; the email that came with a twenty-page guidance file attached. A copy of the guidance is also waiting in the house, the client said; she left it on the coffee table in the front room. She will call, the client said, once she has checked into her hotel in New York.

On the drive from the station, Mercy opens the guidance file on her phone. The client said she would include a list of things to check on the first day. She is scrolling through when the taxi stops. She looks up. It is too soon to stop. Through the windshield, which is blurred with rain, the road is still empty. The house, and its surrounding meadow, has yet to appear. The driver turns back in his seat and says he can go no further. From here on, thanks to the rain, the way up is all mud.

On climbing out, they stand by the boot, squinting in the drizzle.

The driver lifts both cases out, onto the ground beside the verge.

'Here,' he says, with a grimace. 'Will you be all right from here?'

Mercy wipes rain from her eyes. 'Perfect,' she says. 'Thank you.'

Earlier, at the station, when she told him the address, the driver asked if she is related to the woman who lives here. She said no, she is not. She told him she is here for work.

'Yeah?' the driver said. They were in motion then, and his gaze met hers in the mirror. His eyes were deeply set, beneath greying brows.

She said yes; I'm here for work.

He fell quiet for a while, watching the road. Outside, a wall of green was thickening on the right-hand side. On the other, the green was sparse, bursts of shrubs and bushes, broken now and then by the stone walls of gardens and properties.

'So,' the driver said, after a time, 'what is it that you do?'

'I teach – maths,' she said. 'And take photos. Nature photos.'

'Ah, really?' the driver said. 'How interesting.'

'Hoping to take a few more while I'm based here,' she said. 'But I'm here – well, I'm here as I'm housesitting?'

She wasn't sure why the words came out like that. Why her voice tapered up into the tune of a question. As though it is uncertain, yet to be verified. As though she has not lived like this for the past eleven months.

'Right,' he said. And: 'It's a good spot for nature photos. It's not always like this,' with a nod to the windscreen. In the mirror, his face crinkled as he smiled.

Now, out by the car, she hoists her bag up and balances it on top of a suitcase.

The driver says she has his card if she needs help, whether that is for shopping – anything. 'You have my card.'

'For sure,' she says. And then she thanks him again.

He turns and climbs back into his car, and then he is gone and she is alone.

4

Once here, in Meadowlight, after the hike up the road, far from easy with the suitcases and the rain; once here, inside, after the struggle with the door, twisting the key – the beat of dread: is this door stuck, as it was at the stay in Bromley, number six, when the client was reachable, still in the UK, and when it was still possible to call to ask for help, but here, with no locksmiths close, and no neighbours, and the client on a flight – here it was a relief when the door shifted, gave way, and more relief from the warmth on stepping in, and more from the surprise – underfloor heating, a relief for her feet, sore, out of the boots in just her socks; warm, the house, an embrace, as thunder pressed over the roof; once here, in the quiet, she will call Ekua, her mentor, to start.

5

Three people know that for now, this place is hers.

The client
The cab driver
Ekua

Ekua – who she will call now. As has become a tradition.

And the client, for now, does not exist. For as Ekua said: while you are there, the place is yours.

Client: mother of cats, collector, guardian of fish.

It was tough at the start to stay in any house.

Not for the actual work that it takes to keep a house – not for the cleaning, watering plants and watching the pets – rather it was difficult at the beginning because of this: the sense of intruding, when new in a house.

This feeling now, the awareness of a prior fullness to this place, all of which is still here but gone.

At least here, she tells herself, the pets will be quieter. It was hardest to settle in houses where pets wanted to be close. At one house in Islington, a husky had entered the bedroom each night

a pause

and then the mattress sagged with his weight.

The morning after that first night, she called Ekua, ready to quit. It was too much then: the awareness of intruding on someone else's space, and of being responsible for their home.

So far, the feeling is milder here. Perhaps because it is so far from the city. Far from that murmur of background noise, different but steady everywhere. Now, in the stillness, she sheds her coat and hangs it up behind the door. She slips her phone from the pocket, and walks on, down the hallway.

In the front room, as promised, on the table: the guidance pack.

The sofas are different to how they looked last time, on the tour. It takes a moment to realise why. It is the cushions. The cushions have multiplied.

She sits. Takes one cushion onto her lap and rests her arms on it. On her phone she opens the map.

A sea of green surrounds the house.

Ahead, through the bay windows, is the meadow, hazy with rain. Beyond it, the green thickens into woodland.

Judging by the map, the nearest lake is at least an hour away. Unclear how steep the going is from here, whether it will be possible to reach the shore before sunset. With the camera. A first-day photo, to capture this feeling.

6

The beauty of this land, the internet says, is in its movement. Before, this terrain buckled with the heat and tension of its displacement. Craters sank, poured out smoke and liquid rock, and, on cooling, gathered water and snow. Tongues of ice stretched and cracked over the land, swelled in cold, and in warmth thinned into lakes. The land's movement left ripple-contours across the earth.

7

Early in a sit, while the quiet holds this calm, she has made a practice of listing things to try.

Such as:

stretches, following a video sent by a friend
new dishes from local takeaway shops
organic conditioners for wash day

For this house, today, it is a list of recipes. A menu of old dishes, from Sundays cooking with Auntie E. New dishes, too, make this list. Fruit crumbles. Pies.

A surprise – this first-day list. She sits back and looks at it. Still, it feels right, to focus on cooking here. Food, after all, is the centre, and always has been. After this, she adds to the end of the list: take more photos.

The client said no photos may be taken of this house.

Yet.

Here she is, with her cameras. Though not for the house; for the park. For the girls.

If they will come.

⋆

And with the list, here, in the front room, she almost does it. She almost sends the house's location to the girls' chat. It is the quiet, she tells herself; it is because at this moment the rain has stopped. The only movement here now is in the tank, across the room, where three orange fish move back and forth behind the glass.

Here, alongside the list, is the central purpose of these weeks:

watch the fish
keep the house

And watch the cats. Although cats being cats will for the most part watch themselves. One came in not long ago and stretched his warmth against her shin. Ubuntu, judging by the smoky motion of his tail, as her hand smoothed over his fur. The other two are shy; they are still in hiding.

And it is tempting, with this quiet. To invite the girls. To see how they react. It would not be for the first time. The gathering in Ladbroke Grove began in a similar way, sharing a location and then: Heyy, I have a house.

But this one, this house, cannot go like the stay in Ladbroke Grove: board games, charades, pizza, chaos. There, it was the women from the x-kingdom group chat she invited. She sent her location to the group while browsing takeaway menus one night, struck by the scale of savings to be made on group orders, said: Instead of Zoom, why don't we catch up in person?

The response, to her surprise, was confusion. Though the group chat was busy, new questions every other day, they had not seen each other for months by then. Not since the church that had brought them together had collapsed.

'How?' was the response to her suggestion.

And:

'What's happening?'

'Are you OK?'

To which she said, 'Yeah. I have a free house. I'm ordering pizza. It's been ages.'

And, to her surprise, in time, some of them came over. Seven women playing cards and board games in the front room: women who were at least as ruined as she felt, still waking day after day in the shadow of the debt, in the aftermath of the church's unravelling; reeling from the speed with which it had happened, their offerings as investments, all they had given to support the church's growth. The rumours of fraud, and money laundering, and then the collapse, all they had lost within a year, and now what remained, the loans that still needed to be paid off. They needed it – they needed silliness, and space – but opening the door to that house opened the door to more and more, and to the whisky, truth or dare, tequila shots . . . and when the others showed up at ten with ket?

But this – Meadowlight – this one will not end like that stay. She had to pay for a damaged table in that house. It took a month to find a new place after that, with the one-star review the client left on the app. This house will not end on that level. A good review from a place like this will open doors.

She closes the group chat for now, and dials Ekua's number instead.

8

None of these housesits could have happened without Ekua. Though Ekua will say, should this come up when they speak: Nonsense.

She will say this in her Ghanaian auntie accent.

Ekua: big sister, mentor. Poodle-doodler.

Still, it is true, even if Ekua's version is as well.

Sure, this opportunity is all her. She – Mercy – found this house, or it found her. She interviewed and built up reviews through previous sits to stay here. But without Ekua's advice, she might have given up on this months ago.

It might appear to someone who sees life from this perspective – someone like her friend Ife, who may or may not visit during this stay, who spoke in terms of manifestation, of the power – and necessity – of calling dreams into being, of binding things in heaven and thus on earth, of calling into being a life from desire, or belief; and perhaps, in some way, they were the same – from this perspective, it might seem that this house came from hope and belief.

She calls Ekua in the front room, but the signal falters. It is just as poor in the hallway, by the door. Back in the front room, through the window, the rain appears to have stopped. She unpacks her camera from her bag. The signal might be stronger on a walk.

Outside, in the meadow, the air is cool. She looks up at the facade. The house looks just as it first appeared on the app. She was not even looking for a new place when she first noticed it. It was more that it had become routine to check by then, a habit to refresh the app throughout the day. The ratings from the past few sits had been slow to filter in. The number beside her name and photo had not changed in months. With each check, she tried to look at her profile with fresh eyes, too. Her picture: a self-portrait taken with the clicker, on a walk, a clear day in autumn, dog-walking in Finsbury Park. And in that season, in that routine, this house had appeared.

That was in February, which meant the next few sits would be the last with Ekua as a mentor. Soon there would no longer be the option to call her with questions, or simply to chat. To ask for a tour of the house Ekua was sitting at the time. Each tour unfolded in the same way, though each house was new and startling. Ekua, with the phone held out ahead, wearing a robe over a bikini. Year of summer, she had said; she was following the sun around the world. Ekua usually ended those tours by a pool, with a speech – on how all it takes is consistency, and some luck, to build such a life.

Thunder echoes around her. A shiver ripples through the meadow. Rain. More is on the way. The sound patters from every direction. Again, thunder. And now the rain is drilling hard. Ice down her back. Mercy hurries back up the steps into the house.

Inside, she sets the camera on the table in the front room.

It would have been nice to take photos here, inside, while the rain passes. It could have been special on this first day, to capture it – the tranquillity – but the client said it is too soon to take photos in here. She said that despite her work to renovate it, this house is incomplete. Once she returns from the States, she said, that afternoon on the tour, she will continue working on it. She will sort the garden, and the basement, and then she would like to open this place as a retreat. With its location, by the park, and all the art she has gathered here, she said that it would be ideal for visitors.

She said she had not planned to use this property as yet another home. At this, Mercy had offered to take photos during her time here. She had said the photos could help to market it as a retreat. She would have all her lenses, to shoot in the park, anyway. And it would be fun, a new project, to photograph a house like this. She was surprised when the client said no.

Besides the building not being ready, there is the issue of her art collection, the client explained. She wants to share it, but in a particular way, she said. She is protective of the paintings and sculptures she keeps here, some of which are on display throughout the house. With this, the client said she does not want pictures of her house posted online. She does not want any of her art on the internet.

Even uploading pictures of the house onto the app to attract sitters was tough, she said. But she liked the photos, she said, that Mercy emailed after the tour. These were shots from walks and previous sits. The client appreciated them; she said it was part of what made her decide to work with Mercy. She said it was fine to take a few photos here, as long as they did not show too much of the actual house. It was fine to shoot neutral places, background settings, blank walls – windows.

Superstitious, perhaps, but with justification, the client said. This house is important; it is as good as her soul project.

From behind, she hears a sound – a footfall. One of the cats. She walks lightly to the door and peers out. The hallway is clear. She remembers, then, the other photos they discussed. Pet portraits – the client said she had enjoyed those pictures, too. She had liked the photos – mostly of dogs – Mercy had sent. She has very few pictures of her cats. Thinking of them again now, Mercy goes back into the front room. She takes up the camera and loops the strap around her neck. With the rain, now might be a good time to photograph them. Usually it takes a while for pets to get comfortable with her being there. Better to start early, especially with three adult cats.

Moving through the house, there is still no sign of the cats. She takes her laptop, and the camera, up the stairs to the study. Here, also, silence hangs undisturbed. She places her laptop on the desk. Lifts the lid. This matters, too: to set up for work.

The client said the WiFi will be most reliable in this room. She said that this is where she worked, through the pandemic, lecturing.

Mercy rolls the chair back from the desk. The chair is padded, and looks comfortable. The room also looks fine, and now with the rain slashing the windows, it is even cosy in here. A relief. This room will serve as the centre for her stay. From the following morning there will be classes to teach at this desk. She has booked them in, back to back, to fill up the next few days. It is easiest that way; it has helped at previous sits. It helps to start off busy, to maintain the routine.

Now, she sits at the desk to test the camera, the lighting, and the WiFi. The client will call later today, as her email said.

An idea resurfaces, now, as the laptop starts.

The idea is not new. It is a project she has included on first-day lists at previous houses. She has not included it for this stay, but thinking, now, of previous houses, this feels like the best place to try it.

The idea is simple: to record a video.

She looks out through the window. Later, when the rain calms, she could film outside, too.

This idea is from the housesitters' group chat, one that repeats in the back-and-forth of tips for building income streams, remote work; for leaning into what sparks interest, into beauty and health, into fitness, into making; for curiosity, for fun. This idea repeats: to make content, and to start from somewhere interesting.

Start a channel. Make a video, reflect for the camera. (If you build – no, *film* – it, they will come.)

While the laptop connects, she leaves the desk and walks back downstairs. In the front room, she takes the guidance document and unpacks two more lenses.

And walking back up to the study, a script comes together in her mind.

She could film an introduction. A video to explain her journey here. An easy story: how to get into a place like this. Into this life. Into this rhythm of moving from house to house. A choice, to begin with, yet at the same time not. It was a choice in the sense that, yes, there were other options that might have worked. Though even then, at the beginning, with the unease, the sense of intruding, even then, almost a year ago now, this seemed like the best option. The choice was easy, and more so when the house she was renting went up for sale.

She can still remember the shock, how surreal it felt. A housemate had found the page and shared the link in the group chat. The house: there, on Rightmove, before the landlord called to tell them. When he confirmed it, that he was indeed planning to sell, he said he was surprised that they had not seen it coming. The market was recovering, he said; it was the sensible thing to do. And he said he was tired; sure, Tottenham had changed in the past years, but it had not changed enough for him to stay. And the building was old, he said, and in need of renovation.

She remembers the crushing dread of the days that followed. She remembers watching the messages between the other housemates fill their group chat. They were already looking at new houses to rent. They were talking about moving together, as a group. They had full-time jobs. They had healthy credit scores. They had not spent several months taking out loans on behalf of a fraudulent church.

And from there came a choice. She knew that it would be difficult to find another room to rent. Even thinking about it – looking for a place in another house, ideally close enough to keep to the same dog-walking routes – was exhausting. It would be difficult, she knew, while still overwhelmed by the debt, and from the shock of the church's collapse. It had been tough before, with a steady job; it would be impossible with this patchwork of hustles.

★

Housesitting was already an option then. Earlier that winter, she had sat her first two places. Both stays had been favours for friends of friends. She had not sought them out. She had not imagined attempting to sit houses full time. She had stayed at their places to watch their dogs, water their plants, while they travelled for work. But she had read about others who did it as a lifestyle. So by then it seemed possible. Even if it did not work, it promised a break from the house in Tottenham, an escape from the room where, months earlier, her relationship had fallen apart. She needed to get away, out of the room where Gemz had left, with no warning.

At the thought, her throat tightens. She sits forward and strokes the keypad on her laptop. It is too early to let thoughts of Gemz, and the break-up, trickle in. These rooms are clear; they hold no memories of that time. Here is a gift: to start again, again and again.

At the start, in those weeks before, with the house in Tottenham for sale, when couples came up to follow the estate agent through the rooms, and to the garden, she did it then – set up a profile on the app.

A page with information. A selfie. A photo from a walk, with a client's dog in Finsbury Park. A description, age, location, interests, experience – and there, just like that, a new option.

And better still when Ekua appeared, an experienced sitter, with advice, on YouTube. After an exchange of messages, Ekua added her to the WhatsApp group chat, a network of women sharing tips, as they moved from house to house.

At the time there were other options – that much is true. Good options, too, all of which offered chances to reconnect. They all offered ways to reach out to friends and relatives again. The first option, then, was to stay with Sammi, in Cricklewood. And the idea had warmed her, more than the others at the time. She had wanted to reach out after so long, to ask to return to that house for a few months. She missed the community and purpose about that place. The calm, inside, after the bustle of the high road. She missed Sammi, above all else, her company, her humour, their easy bond.

Alas. She knew that if she got a place it could only be for a short time. It was close to winter then, which meant the rooms would be occupied. This was fair. It meant the house was working as Sammi had intended. Better, perhaps. Other women needed that house more. She had only secured a bed there in the first place from the winter she had stayed to help. When Sammi had first opened it, she had helped set up. She can still picture Sammi by the sink, biting her lip, the resolve in her gaze. The housewarming: bring a dish that tastes like home. She had brought a tray of waakye, covered in foil. After that night, it was hard to leave. The work kept her: cleaning up, making brunch, helping Sammi assemble furniture. Painting the hallway, cooking, and taming the wilderness behind the house. It made sense to sleep over, so she did, and Cricklewood became home. Weeks became months; time lost its meaning in that house. Sammi, who made a shelter out of her uncle's HMO.

Another option at the time was to stay in Wood Green, with Auntie E, who had said, in simpler times, she was always welcome. They were family. Her home was theirs. Auntie E, mother's cousin, in a one-bed flat in Wood Green. With the sofa bed in the front room. Staying there would have been less of an imposition than staying in Cricklewood. Besides, she could have helped. Auntie E was still recovering months after her fall. Although the fall was not a fall, she said; she had only slipped. She had slipped on an escalator at King's Cross on her way home from work.

Auntie E, Mother said, on a call one afternoon, your auntie still won't leave her flat. We went and we waited and knocked – she is not coming out. Try and speak to her, please. Mercy. I'm asking you.

So she went to see, and there, in Wood Green, the church situation began.

Though it did work, in a sense – visiting her. For tradition, she bought a tub of rainbow ice cream on the way, though it was really just the three shades – chocolate, strawberry, vanilla – no true rainbow. Still, tradition, from nights when the parents had to work late, and years after when Auntie E left her husband: buy ice cream, stay in, watch a film.

That day, she arrived with ice cream, and buzzed at the entrance. When no answer came, she tailed a person in through the doors and up the stairwell, and then she knocked and knocked.

And it worked.

After a film, they went out for a walk. Though heading back, by the crossing, Wood Green being Wood Green, a preacher approached them. He stood alone, his gaze fixed on them as they crossed the street. He had been speaking into a microphone and offering leaflets to passers-by, but now he paused his sermon and put the microphone into a pocket of his corduroy jacket. Mercy knew what was coming, but Auntie E seemed interested. They stayed and listened as he reminded them that Jesus loved them. Before they left, he gave them leaflets – invitations. A church nearby, he said, going through a revival. 'Don't miss out on your blessing,' he said.

Back in the flat, Auntie E put the leaflet on her fridge. 'I will see you next Sunday, then,' she said. 'Or are you busy?'

With that, and what had followed in the churches they moved on to, to return to stay with Auntie E was no real option. By then, Auntie E seemed to be deep in her new church. Her faith was back with a fervency neither of them had known before. There would have been questions, had Mercy gone to stay with her, and she would have had to explain about her own new church and its collapse. And the debt.

Her third option, back then, was to reach out to the girls, to take them up on their promise.

The girls from Enfield: Ife, Bessie and Joy. A sisterhood that stretched back to the years before primary school, the playdate that had brought them together in the park one Saturday. Theirs was a deliberate loyalty, closeness that grew over the years. They had nurtured it, through sleepovers as well as school. From that sisterhood came a wealth of promises, some childish, others impossible. But among them was a promise always to make time for sleepovers. Which, in practice, meant always to offer a place for each other to crash.

Their mothers had encouraged them to look out for each other. They said, from here, life could take them anywhere. The girls were the first of their lines to be born here, in the UK. As long as you study hard, their mothers told them, the world is yours, but it won't be easy. You have to fight for it. They had to try, their mothers told them, to help each other to flourish. And for a while, they had; for a while it was easy.

So, in Tottenham, after the break-up and the return to church, and with the debt from the church's collapse, she thought to use this moment to reach out – to end the silence that had kept them distant since uni. It had changed them, leaving Enfield; she felt it, and at the time she was afraid to see how much. She thought to ask to stay with one of them for a few nights. Even if it meant enduring their mothers' I-told-you-sos.

She looked on their socials, to see where they were. She wanted to get a sense of what the years had made of them. To her relief, they were still in London.

Ife: a lawyer
Bessie: in corporate banking, engaged
Joy: running her own development consultancy

On reading this, happiness bloomed inside her chest. A win for one – or three – was a triumph for all of them. But with that, it felt unthinkable to reach out. She could not bring herself to message them, as she was, to confess to existing within this mess, twenty-six, jobless, and as good as homeless then. She could not bring herself to talk through the chain of mistakes that had led her here. And worse – the realisation of how far away they were. Despite all they had endured together through school, and even with their mothers' prayers and encouragement, over the years they had grown into strangers. She scrolled through their socials for a while, clicking back through their photos. The girls were only faces on a screen. Four years had passed since they had been together in one place. It was then that she understood how small her world had become. And with this, housesitting, the WhatsApp group promised a way out.

Perhaps she will tell the story of this path to here at some point, present it as part of a video. Here, in this house, or in the park – a fine backdrop. But not today.

A message flashes on her phone screen. Ekua – asking if she is in her new place yet. And did she try to call earlier?

9

The job of a housesitter is to help clients to relax. But at its best, the arrangement enables mutual relaxation.

Ekua says this again, as they speak over the phone. They keep it brief, a tradition to mark the start of each new sit. She has to go, Ekua says after less than two minutes on the call. Enjoy yourself. We'll speak again soon. Remember, it's all about relaxation.

She first said this months ago, on one of their early calls, back when she was pitching this arrangement as a way to reach for something more. Housesitting is not just about temporary convenience, she said. This is important work – meaningful work. For what could be more important, she said, than peace of mind?

With each stay, the client benefits from knowing their home and pets are in good hands. As simple as it sounds, it means a great deal to clients, she said. It gives them permission to stay away, while they travel; it allows them to switch off and remain present where they want to be. And in return, the sitter benefits too. They get chill-time. Pet therapy. A break from paying rent.

With the savings, she has been eating better – while

chipping away steadily at the debt. And here, after the call, she cooks her first proper meal in months. If there is a place to cook again, it is here, in Meadowlight. This house has two and a half kitchens. The half: an outdoor grill and oven from the client's ex-husband.

It feels strange to set vegetables out on the worktop in the kitchen. Before this stay, there have been months of existing on takeaways at past houses, takeaways and ready meals and easy-to-clean tray-bake dishes, efficient meals that made sense in the city; it seemed reasonable, then, to minimise kitchen time, and with that to reduce the risk of provoking the fire alarm. Neighbours at one sit complained – an over-sensitive alarm and the oven there blackened with grease that no amount of scrubbing would shift.

Here in Meadowlight there are no restaurants for miles. Going by the map on her phone, the closest looks like it is in a pub. So she cooks. She slips back into the rhythm of unpacking groceries that she bought by the station, stocking the fridge and the cupboard over the sink. Later, she will buy more. She will need to buy more in order to cook fuller meals again, and to try out new dishes over the coming weeks. For now though, there are enough ingredients to make something basic. It is easy from here. Muscle memory. Comforting, too, to wash and slice real food again. Fried rice with the chicken, and the eggs in their carton on the top shelf of the fridge.

Most of the recipes on the list that she has left in the front room are from gentle days cooking with Auntie E, and later, from that summer in Cape Coast, at the chop bar Auntie E had opened before she left Ghana.

The rice turns out well – she puts the leftovers in Tupperware in the fridge.

Day one, she sits at the table in the dining room to eat. On the tour, the client said she designed this room for hosting. The room: wooden table, oval, curving with the walls, with the light feature – shards of stained glass and wooden blocks – from Marrakesh. A whole room for hosting. And drinking, the client said. A friend used to visit; they sat for hours here, drinking wine.

She has found, on previous sits, it takes three days to relax into a new place. Three days to feel settled enough to sleep through the night. It is easiest to settle in when those first days are open, when she is free to focus on the work, on teaching as usual, with minimal interruptions.

So. When the client emails to ask when she would next like to check in, Mercy suggests day four. The client has said she would like to be able to speak on a video call next time. She has been struggling, she wrote, with the hotel WiFi. They spoke on day one, as agreed, in the evening, and though they only spoke over the phone, the call lasted longer than either of them had expected.

The client emails back within minutes.

Yes, she says. They can speak the following day. She needs time to recover from her journey, which, she adds, must have been clear from their first call. From her rambling, and the terrible WiFi. Next time, she writes, WiFi permitting, they will speak on a video call.

Ideally, Mercy thinks now, the cats will be up here by then as well. The client will have missed them and will appreciate seeing them. She sits up and looks around the study.

So far, the cats have been evasive. They are everywhere in the house that she is not. They emerge when she is here in the study – they come out to eat. Once she is back up here, with their bowls refilled, the cycle restarts.

The first call with the client was meant to be a quick check-in, to confirm her arrival. But it unspooled into a longer conversation. On the phone, the client said over and over that she was sorry. Sorry about the chaos with which this call was unfolding. Sorry to have called half an hour later than she had said she would.

She said she had forgotten the toll that flying took. Now it was catching up, she said, exhaustion, in her room above Times Square, with the light and noise outside the window.

She would have preferred to speak on a video call, she said. Phone calls were too formal. She only spoke on the phone when all other efforts had failed, to pay a bill or to cancel a subscription. There was an anonymity to audio-only calls she disliked. Anyway, she was disappointed, she said, because she had hoped to speak on video regularly, though she understood it might not be typical – 'What is normal, here?' she asked.

Mercy said that it varies. There are no rules. Most clients do not feel the need to check in so often. The client said, then, in that case, it would likely help her more than it would benefit Mercy.

She went on to say that her luggage had been lost. She had given up on waiting at baggage reclaim, taken a cab from the airport through Manhattan, and checked into her hotel. She was distracted, as she had put her notebook – with the lines for her speech – in the bag that was now missing. She had hoped to use these days to learn those lines, and rest, to prepare the speech she was due to give.

Mercy listened in surprise. Never had she encountered a client who had so much to say.

She said that she had moved the notebook to the hold at the last minute, decided to take it from her carry-on bag in the hope it would allow those words to set – after all, she intended to work on them later; so, the book of notes – for her speech at the university in three weeks, the speech which up till then she had foolishly only written out by hand; although it was not foolish, at the time, she said, to write like that, it was only a mistake now her luggage was lost.

The speech was important, she said; it would be her most personal yet. It was hers, not for an institution. Her days in academia were already over by the time the invitation arrived. The speech was hers, to discuss her practice and approach. Not just to reflect on art and repatriation; this was a chance to talk about her life as a collector. So as she spoke on the call on that first night, this: a tangent from an apology, her voice softened. She told Mercy of how the speech had come together, how hard it had been to stop writing it at times, that she did not stop, once she was in flow, she did not stop till it was there across the page, tangled and messy, sure, but there.

How easy she said, for passion to spiral out of control.

As though to demonstrate this, she went on about writing. Said that the idea of writing by hand had always seemed more honest. There was, she said, symmetry in writing like this, writing as she had begun, with a pen, as though nothing had changed since her student years. She had started writing notes as an archive for her collection, an act of gratitude, in recognition, she said. She kept the notes to acknowledge each piece she acquired, and to note its significance. To write was to make sense of a piece, she said, to register its existence in the library of the mind, and to open it to future connections. So for each piece she wrote her thoughts on its significance, on its value to the cultures to which it belonged. These notes, she said, became a blog, for she was aware then of the precarity of handwritten notes, how easily they could be lost. And in time that blog became the book, but even then, she still liked to write her notes by hand. It was grounding, she said, to sit at the desk to write.

Thinking over it again, here in the study at the desk, returns the memory of those scribbled notes from before. Mercy can picture them now, the notes she and Gemz used to write by hand, scraps of poetry from their back-and-forth. She presses her palms on the cool surface of the desk. She remembers, too, how their exchange of fragments began – with her idea of adding lyrics to one of Gemz's tracks. She remembers the piece Gemz played on loop one evening, as they walked through Covent Garden. She was thinking about shooting photos there with the lights, capturing something new in the busyness. She wanted to absorb the setting first, to wander through it and take in the atmosphere.

'Every place needs its soundtrack, you know?' Gemz said then. She was listening to music on a phone that she carried at all times solely for music. They were listening together, through one earphone each.

'Uhh. Every place?' she said.

'Hundred per cent,' Gemz said.

They stepped around a group of tourists who had stopped for a photo.

'I mean, doesn't every place already have its own soundtrack?' Mercy said.

Gemz said maybe. Actually, yeah, that was true. In a way. She said she reckoned that most places had multiple soundtracks. She slowed down, as she thought about it.

'But I mean like something more,' Gemz said after a while. 'Well, not more – it is simpler. Like something that distils the place – if you get it.'

'Umm.'

'Maybe something that reflects what's underneath a place.' Then she said, 'OK, just listen to this, please. I think when you hear it you will hear it.'

They walked on listening to the soundtrack Gemz had made for Covent Garden. In the sound, she felt closer to the memories that were layered over the streets.

'We used to come to this sweetshop on Saturdays,' Mercy said. They had stopped in the pink glow of a glass-fronted shop. A neon sign was flashing above the open door. 'My dad worked here, for the longest time. Security. The guy in the sweetshop let us fill our bags for free.'

Then came the memory of how it had felt here, as a kid. Bundled in cotton, in matching coats and hats with her sister, Efia. Taking photos on the disposable camera, trying to get the street performers in the background in the frame. Sweetness ringing in the throat on the tube home. And then years later, here again, after uni. It was here, one afternoon, walking alone, she had seen a poet. From the fervency of the voice she had at first thought it was a preacher. And then something about the rhythm of her words had snagged back time. University. Spoken word. A girl in a shawl glimmering. The tone was too raspy, the woman's height and all her gestures were off, yet everything inside her chest had pressed up, gathered taut, ready to break. And then came the relief, because it was not her. It was not the poet she had in mind, from university. Another woman. Another poet.

This came out, too, on that evening walk with Gemz. She realised what was missing about the track.

'I think I get it,' she said. 'But you should write something for this, too.'

'I should write something?'

'Poetry would be so good – it would be chef's kiss over these tracks.'

In the weeks that followed, she started writing lines herself. At Gemz's place in Willesden Green, before the split, and months before the church, before the house in Tottenham went up for sale, before the panic and then before this housesitting, before: in the season too delicate to recall here. She remembers pages of words in her pockets folded small, over and over, pages tucked into pockets that appeared the morning after, when pulling on last night's clothes in the stillness of Gemz's place.

To think of that, here, is too much. Too soon. There will come a time to tease these memories apart. This house has room enough to try.

10

On day four, before their call, the client sends another email.

Mercy opens it at the desk, while rain patters on the window.

Class is still happening on the laptop; twelve students in three rows of individual squares are working through a problem set. The A-level algebra class allows room for multitasking, so she scrolls through the client's email on the second screen.

The message is a flow of sentences circling over themselves. The gist is there from the first line: the client is asking about the cats.

Mercy sits forward. She reads the email again. She has not thought about the cats, about getting them together in one place, seriously, until now.

The client writes that she misses them – horribly.

These past four days, she writes, are the longest she has ever spent away from them. She is looking forward to seeing them on the video call tonight.

Mercy cracks her knuckles over the keyboard. This is important, to reassure the client. She types a response.

Hiya, sure. No problem. Looking forward to speaking with you soon too!

With this sent, she rests both elbows on the desk by the laptop. Presses her palms against her cheeks. There is a tremor in her wrists. Her pulse is in her fingertips, harder in her thumbs. And beyond, apart from her own life, all is still. Silence rings through the study. Through the house.

It should be easy to find three missing cats. Which is not to suggest they are missing. They could be outside, in the garden.

She has not even looked for them yet, not properly. She has left them to their routines, to accept her presence in their own time. She has made no further effort beyond leaving their food out in the hallway.

After class ends, she will look for them properly. She will call Ekua again, too. Ekua always knows what to do.

11

The cats were comfortable the first time she met them here, on the tour.

Ubuntu
Oyo
Sankofa

The client had invited her to see how well they would get on, and to decide whether Mercy, too, would get on in this place. A remote house is not for everyone, she said. She was surprised, the client said, by the number of people interested in staying. More so since the photos she had posted were so bad.

They are abysmal, she said, that day, and winced. There is no need to be polite.

It was true. The photos were tilted, unfocused, blurred at their edges, and in some the client's shadow fell into the frame. None of the photos captured the atmosphere in here. The client said she had taken them in a rush.

She would not say how many people were interested, although Mercy asked.

Enough, she said, to guarantee she would find someone

decent. At least one candidate was sure to get on with the cats. The cats were particular, she said; four weeks was a long time.

She said that she had wondered if sitters might prefer to work together here. On looking at other houses on the app, she had wondered if Meadowlight might be too much.

Mercy felt grateful then for Ekua and the network. Ekua had said this was part of why she had started the community: the possibility of making friends through housesitting. Plenty of couples did it together, she said, friends too. It would help them learn from and support each other. She had doubled up on housesits with women in the network herself at times. She said she liked to help directly in matchmaking. It came naturally as she had worked with most of them at some point; she had a good sense for who might get on.

Growing up, this is the community I dreamed of, Ekua said in a YouTube video. So many of us want to connect. We're so scattered. So even if you're in a house on your own, with us, you're never alone.

At the house, when Mercy met the cats, the client had given her a tour. The tour had been an interview that unfolded from room to room; a conversation that branched and twisted back. Mercy only realised it had been the interview when they were back by the front door.

The client said that she preferred to interview people while walking – the housekeeper, the gardener, the painter – she said she had always found walking meetings more insightful. She had found walking in general essential to clear the head.

★

'It is well known by now that we are too sedentary,' she said. 'We know it, and yet, so far, no change. Not a good sign for us. As a species.'

At the time, in the kitchen, Mercy agreed. She leaned back, against the worktop by the sink. Said she had started housesitting in part because of the need to walk, which had arisen from weeks of walking dogs.

The client looked up from the glasses she had set on the counter. Oh, she said, you're a dog person.

12

She may well be a dog person, Mercy thinks now, in the study. Especially given how these cats have reacted to her so far. As though they can tell. She had asked Ekua, at the start, on a call months before: Is it worth focusing on staying in houses with dogs first? Would it make sense to build up experience and reviews based on what comes naturally?

After all, her experience with pets had begun with dogs. Amber-lit afternoons around Alexandra Palace. Aside from the animals on the farm back in Kumasi, on long summer breaks, the pigs and goats and turkeys with their noise, and the chickens pecking their way through the compound, her experience with creatures beyond dogs was limited.

Ekua's answer was: It depends.

'Honestly, there are no rules to this thing, right? But. I would say it is best not to restrict yourself. That's part of the beauty of housesitting,' she said. 'You get to try out so many things, with no pressure to commit. So hey, why not. You never know what you might be good at until you try. I guess that's why you wanted to work with me, though?' she said. 'For more places with dogs?'

*

In truth, she had reached out to Ekua in the first place, through YouTube, due to her name. She had messaged her from the relief of finding another Ghanaian in this, sitting houses – nice houses, too, travelling. Although, sure, Ekua had grown up not in London like she had, but in Amsterdam. She said, 'I've never even actually been to London, would you believe?' when Mercy asked her where in London she was based. If anything, Ekua said, London was at the bottom of her list. The city itself was fine, she added; a place so vast and full had to be complex in good ways, too. It wasn't the idea of the city itself that she disliked, she said, the issue was more about how being there seemed to alter people, ossified them; how the city – its rhythm, its impatience – took their softness. Besides, she said, the place was overhyped.

From the videos she had posted, Ekua was clearly a dog person. Her channel consisted of footage of various dogs, of all breeds and sizes. She had posted videos on walks with them, washing them, trimming their coats, and longer videos reviewing accessories. Ekua: poodle-doodler, was her online name; a name she said had stuck from her original channel, animations she had made – doodles of dogs shaped like clouds, mini-clouds atop their heads and tails. When they met, for the first time, on an introductory video call, one of the first things Ekua said was that she had always wanted to work with dogs.

This had resonated with Mercy, to her surprise. It made sense given the relief of those autumn walks, the simplicity, the calm of that season in Haringey. The feeling is still here, a tingling in the chest, and beneath: that undertow, that counterflow, as heavy as regret. Though Ekua was right that at the time, yes, it would have been limiting, still, sticking to dogs would have been simpler, would have prevented this from happening.

Dog-walking became her reason to venture out, from the end of that summer in which the church collapsed. Those weeks were restorative. For one, they brought security – a friend of an ex-flatmate's cousin needed a dog-walker, and offered to pay. And the thought of the dog waiting, tail flicking, in those weeks was enough reason to leave bed each day, to climb out and brave the shower, with its chill, its sputtering – and to face the wardrobe, the mess of old clothes bundled there, to pull on jeans, a top and a coat and then go out.

That season became the start of this new second life. That time of walking through parks led her back to rediscovering her cameras and taking photos again. A new project, and an offer for clients: to photograph their dogs outside. With that came the afternoon trip back to the flat – back to Enfield, for the first time in a year – back one afternoon to find Efia, still in, alone, having moved back after graduating from uni, little Efia, already working in her first job, now with the room they used to share all to herself. Efia opened the door as she approached, stepped aside to let her in. She backed against the wall, watching as though she was a hologram. Only on realising she was there to grab more stuff did Efia speak. 'You can move back in, you know?' she said.

And the weight of it – so many responses closed her throat. It would have taken more patience than she had to try to explain why she could not.

So she focused on the reason that had brought her back to the flat, went to their room and gathered the lenses, and, back in the hallway, told Efia to let it go. It was natural – healthy – for people to grow, leave home, she said. She told Efia that she was making more of it than it needed to be.

And on leaving again, with the lenses and the quiet, the autumn that followed was kind – gentle. The memory of those last weeks in Tottenham still brings warmth, that time of walking in the glow against the colours of fallen leaves. Those weeks were the beginning of the age of takeaways, too, looking back now; every habit has its root, has its purpose from its time. That was the season of walking back by the parade to buy chips wrapped in paper, thick cut, soft and sure as childhood, with the warmth of long coach journeys to the beach, with friends – brothers and sisters – from a simpler church.

And soon after, more dog-walking jobs came, and then more still from updating her website, and from adding the photos she had taken on those walks.

Ekua once said her calling is to help women realise their dreams.

'I love meeting people who are creative as well,' she said. 'It's the same to me; it all connects – mentoring, art. It's the same. We create possibilities, when we pour into each other's cups.'

Her story is there in full, in a video series on YouTube. Sharing her journey felt important too, she said. She is thirty-one now and considers herself a pioneer, a member of the first generation to grow up on social media. She says that for her, it has been positive. She started with MySpace before vlogging on YouTube. Made it into a portal, through which to share more of her truth, to share it with people she could not find in her life offline. Said that this openness and connection will be the start, that this is the beginning of the shift to change the world. The internet, in her eyes, is a mirror that confronts the world with itself.

In her own story, one of the first videos that Mercy watched, as directed – please watch from the start, from my introductions playlist first – Ekua describes herself as a wandering Ghanaian. She was born in Kumasi, where she lived until she was four, though her memory of the city is dim and fading. Her early memories are of Amsterdam, where she grew up. Coming of age, she succumbed to stories that she knew were not hers. It was easier, she said, at first to follow a well-trodden path, and so she had attempted to live up to expectations that she knew could never fit. Her arc was something of a cliché; she called it a typical beginning for first-born daughters of immigrants. She even read medicine (would you believe it, right?), though not from pressure, but from her own interest. She had wanted to understand it, and then to heal, to comprehend the body and, through that, to fathom life; life: the meaning through which a body reshaped itself. After graduating, seven years in, she realised she had no desire to work in it. So, she said, she quit and retrained as a vet, then found work in dog grooming. It was still care, she said, still healing in some way. If anything, it was a more holistic approach. She broadened her understanding of care to cover expression and joy, to include beauty as well as physical health. With that, she expanded her YouTube channel to reflect the shift.

It was important to start with this, she said, to showcase

the whole route. To acknowledge the turning-back, the meandering that led to here. The doubt, the questioning. The many paths and U-turns that led to a fuller life. That regardless of setbacks, there is always another way.

13

The last exercise of the day, in which all twelve students sit, heads down, writing out their answers and reasoning by hand – this part of class is a good time to check the phone.

She takes it from the second shelf, here, beneath the desk. The screen is a mirror, black, filling now with her face. Her face yet not. Distorted, here her face looks closer to Father's. As at the fair years ago, in Oak Hill Park, the day tinted purple with her shades, Efia in tow, making their way through the haunted mansion. It was her favourite part of the carnival each year – for this, its endless surprises, the warped sheets of mirror, every movement transfigured: Father's smile, a tilt of the head and there appeared Father's mother. Arch of an eyebrow and father's sister, Auntie Bernice. And more, and more, and the thrill of it, the shine in Efia's gaze, her laughter, and later it took only a twitch of a muscle to allude to this memory, a language of recognition between them.

And here again, these reflections, with the phone.

First she checks: the girls' group chat, and yes, here, it is still alive. The chat with Ife, Bessie and Joy. It resurfaced a month ago, when Bessie shared a paragraph announcing her engagement. Bessie, soon to marry a friend she had met at uni. Her on-and-off, was how she described him. Twice as goofy as she is.

Little Bessie, who used to help them all with their maths homework. Who buried herself in maths, committed to it intentionally. Because it was clear, she said, answers were either wrong or right. You could improve, and when you did, if you made progress, anyone could see. Maths, she said, was like polishing a foggy lens – it was possible to see more clearly with each attempt, to improve, to know better with each return. Bessie's devotion to maths unlocked the back-corridor rooms at school. Their teacher, Mr Watts, said they could stay in and use the board – yes, he agreed, it helped to write equations out large, it was easier like that, to solve them and wipe them clear, then start again. So they had the option to stay in during lunch breaks thanks to Bessie, inside away from the gossip and the cold. The room was theirs, as long as they used it to study, and it helped Mr Watts, too, it improved his class average score, as long as they were quiet, and sensible with it. He trusted them, he said, they were brilliant, bright things lay ahead of them. So they stayed in, and Bessie worked through maths problems on the board. She taught them the beauty of integration, all you could tell about the shape of a curve from the numbers, coefficients and constants that shifted the lines. Bessie, in flow, her eyes shining with truth.

'Can't wait for you to meet him,' her last message in the chat reads.

There have been no further details since. The wedding date is yet to be confirmed. But Bessie wanted them to know early, she said, so they could help her plan.

'Yeah, it's been ages,' her message said. 'Been forever. I

know we need to catch up properly. But you girls have been here since the beginning, for real, and we did promise to plan our weddings together. Remember?'

Reading that weeks earlier, the memory made her smile, and now again, at the desk, the thought brings warmth. But it brings sadness, too. Now there may only be room to recognise blessings such as this. Only to acknowledge what has gone well, the successes. As it went with those relatives who, in her childhood, she swore never to become. They were relatives who only appeared when they had good news to share, whose hardships only existed after they had passed, only when they could be presented as testimonies, more evidence of the Lord's favour in their lives.

Still. It was sweet that Bessie remembered. From the time when promises formed as easily as thoughts. Age of dreams, of sleepovers and photo shoots.

At least for now, the old chat is back. And after tonight's call, after asking the client if it is all right for people to visit, as long as the answer is yes, she will invite the girls. It will be something to see how they have changed. If Bessie still loves maths, or if that has waned, now that she works in finance. If she is still trying to map people out in numbers, too, as she did, for a while, in her astrology phase. The flirtation which, on being discovered by their mothers, got her and Ife grounded for a week, and her, Mercy, ushered to the front in church, to that opening between the stage and the congregation, for prayer, intercession – a situation which was as good as an intervention, her skin aflame from the spectacle of it as she stood there at the front, oil cool on her forehead, so many hands in the sanctuary raised, pointed her way, she and the others up in need of protection, although she was still thankful in that, through the embarrassment, grateful then for the sense of being held, the sense, with that, of walking a delicate line, where to lean too far in any direction elicited this, dozens of hands directing prayers into one. What Bessie will say when she finds out that maths has, in a way, served as the foundation of this new life. Teaching these classes has kept her afloat, has set the rhythm of each day; a rope to grasp in that free fall after leaving uni, just as Bessie said it would be.

Today, as usual, the girls' chat is quiet. There is only a link to an article from Ife, an update on a celebrity trial, the kind of drama Ife lived for back in school. Even a hint of scandal would be enough to set her off then, the smallest controversy and she would play devil's advocate for weeks. And to call her shallow would only make her double down. It was a sport to her. She could argue a case from all sides.

'You're missing the point,' she'd say, if anyone called her out. 'It's not that I look at celebrities as role models or anything like that. It's more—' and here she broke off, and frowned. It was as though she was having another debate inside, and then, after a moment, she nodded and continued. 'It's more that I see them – celebrities, I mean – as free. By free I mean, like, unconstrained? They don't have to live by the usual rules, you get? It's interesting, that's all I'm saying, what they can make of it.'

Ife's interest in celebrities always surprised them when it flared up. In everything else, she was the most rational, most clear-sighted. It was she who kept them together and on time, and she who filled in the details of their plans. She held them to account on past promises. It surprised them, the energy she devoted to following celebrity drama, yet it made sense, as superficial as it seemed. The chaos and flamboyance of their lives offered a contrast to the women in her church. To the future and ideals they represented. Ife, who said she did not want to have children when she grew up. The idea of motherhood terrified her, it always had, the disruption that it would bring; she feared that raising other people would pin her down.

A memory: Ife, in her bedroom, back in Enfield, in music, the two of them flicking through the latest edition of *Vogue*. Those Sunday afternoons, when she kept her jewellery on from church, and when Ife and her mother came over to the flat. On those Sundays, Ife stayed instead of joining her mother for more church. Ife's mother was already senior in the women's fellowship by then, and at times she stayed out for multiple services. So those Sundays went with Ife playing Mary Mary CDs on the stereo in her room, discussing the women in the photos in *Vogue*. They bought the magazine with Mercy's allowance from her father, the allowance he gave her to buy copies of *National Geographic*. For inspiration, Father said, to study the photos that had made the cut. And it was fun to travel through those pages. Now that Father had less time to sit with her and read, she picked up a copy of *Vogue* from the off-licence, *Vogue* and Haribo Starmix for Efia – the big packet, to get her to leave the bedroom on those Sundays when Ife came over.

They were happy then; they had all that they could have wanted. The flat felt like paradise, like the centre of the world. She could not have imagined that years later, she would leave it so abruptly. And with the images in the magazine – outrageous, beyond this world, photos of beautiful dresses, beautiful women – the future shimmered with more joy to come. She suspected that for Ife it was not just about the women in those photos, not just about the celebrities, their drama and the openness of their lives, but it was also the fashion that intrigued her. For it was Ife who taught the rest of them to gel their hair back, taught them to contour their make-up and to line their eyes. In time she led them to the salon in Turnpike Lane for their first professional relaxers, perms that left their hair glossy and smooth for a while, and years later it was Ife, too, who sent style ideas for their natural hair transitions.

Mercy sinks her hand into the softness of her hair now.

At times the weight of these thoughts, these memories, presses heavy.

She taps away from the group chat. There are new messages in the housesitters' chat. Welcome messages for two women who joined earlier. She types a welcome message, trails it with emojis and taps send.

New messages await in the x-kingdom chat, too. Only a few. She sits back, relieved. It is time to shift her attention away from this chat. Or at least to balance it out with new conversations. It is time to reach out to friends who fell away while she was in that church – or not quite, not fell away, for the silence was more than that. The silence was intentional, and the distance around her came from an active choice. It is time to reach out to friends she stopped speaking to while she was in the church, as the pastors had instructed. Unsaved people could distract from, and dilute, divine purpose. Friendships outside the church were a danger – and a betrayal. The enemy used non-believers to lead the faithful away from the truth. Still, it is hard, even now, to pull away from the group, more so as someone here might find a way to help them all. If there is a way out, a way to push back at the debt, it is most likely to work if they stand together. Still, too much time here reading this chat and hope diminishes.

Soon, someone will suggest another meeting – another call – and they will return to trade memories about the church. Theories as to how it unravelled.

But it will not help to think about that now. She leaves the app to check for missed calls.

Today, there is just one, from her mother.

At the sight, a slow ache kneads her stomach.

She places the phone on the desk by the laptop. Hard to tell whether Mother meant to call this time, if she dialled and gave up after a few rings, perhaps changed her mind, or had to take another call, or if instead she even called by accident. She has said that this has happened in the past; I didn't mean to call, she said, the last time Mercy called back, I was just looking at your photo, it's a nice photo, I was just looking.

Today, it is just this. The missed call. No voicemail.

Something constricts in her chest. Perhaps tonight she will call back. Try again.

She glances back up to the screen, where the students are still working. A student in the bottom corner lifts his face. It is rare – for a student to look up directly like this, to burn his gaze through the camera. Worry blanches his face. Then, just as quickly, the expression fades, and his gaze shifts again.

Under the desk, she types a message to Ekua.

Heya. Can you speak at 6ish (UK time)? x

14

Likely, the client will say yes to hosting company.

On the tour, she said guests are welcome. Fine. She said that this house gets lonely after a while.

She also said this will be her first time working with a sitter.

She had not heard of housesitting before, not on this scale.

She had learned of it only recently from a friend, who had told of an encounter with a couple in town. A dark-haired woman and a man with a beard. They were young, she said, which alone made them stand out, and then there was the camera and microphone the woman held. Large backpacks were slung from their shoulders.

Her friend had asked them if they were looking for directions. To which they had said no, but then again, perhaps they were. They were travelling, they told her, filming their way across Europe. The journey was the purpose, so they were open to directions. They were travelling to make up for time they had lost inside. Said they had been in their mid-twenties when the pandemic began. They had saved to travel around Europe before Brexit. Now they were here, after the lockdowns, to see as much as they could. They saved on costs by living in people's homes. Not just living, but by caring for pets as well. They watered plants, cleaned each house like it was theirs.

They asked if they could interview her that day, to film her answers for a YouTube channel.

The client frowned as she told Mercy this. 'Hope you don't plan to do that – interview people – here,' she said.

They were here, in this study, when she said this. One of the cats, Ubuntu, was sprawled on his back on the rug, grooming himself.

The rainy light had cast the client's face in gloom: shadows made her features chiselled, stern. Then it surfaced, or it was more that it reappeared, because it had been there before, even if only tentatively. It was a look Mercy had first noticed in the front room, where the client had paused to show her a photo – an image on card, in black and white, a woman: a grandmother – the client said Mercy reminded her of. The resemblance was there, though faint: a familiarity in the shape of her face, and the fall of her gaze. Benin, the client said, her grandmother lived in Benin. She said Mercy's picture on the app resembled her. Based on that, she was sure they would get on.

The resemblance was in the client's face, too, in the study; there for a moment, then the light shifted, her face softened, and it was gone.

A shadow of something harsher tainted her face. A thought or memory weighing on her. She turned away and folded her arms. 'I will never understand the need to broadcast one's life online.'

15

Mercy pushes her chair back from the desk. She is losing track of time here. Once class is through, before looking for the cats, it will help to refresh with a bath.

It has helped in previous sits, when memories have intruded in this way, when a new place becomes disorientating. And there is still time, she tells herself, to look for the cats after a bath.

The bath: a way out from the busyness of work, from the time that runs from morning up to now, from the first coffee to the last class here at the desk. It helps to soak in the water after these back-to-back lessons: complex numbers, integration, trigonometry. Most days will go like this, class after class, with the students, in new permutations, mosaicking across the screen. It is easy to imagine how, within this, three cats might disappear. Class after class – to chip back at the debt, a rhythm that

pauses

at noon, for lunch, half an hour in the kitchen to scoop leftovers, the rice, splash it and microwave it, and then boil an egg at the stove, wipe surfaces with a cloth, and then to sit with her food and open a new browser – a separate window to check the news, and the weather, and to plan the next walk – and then to close it, and go to the real window, the physical one. To stand before the glass – and if the day has already thickened its light away, to look over the garden, and confirm the world still exists. Then back to the desk and the next class.

And now, just thinking of bathing: the ease begins.

Water: running back, up, along a motherline, women immersed, in and beside water; women moving their limbs through the flow, at times in darkness, other times under the sun – so it will go in these moments, in walking back through the room.

It will be after bathing, returning, wrapped in a fresh towel, thickness folded over, as was fun to do on sleepovers – to try what could not fit, pieces and lengths that could only hold them for a while, whose textures belonged to years to come, knowing they could not hold, the relief: to slip them off, forget, try them on again, laugh, shed them and try again, a game of becoming more; and fun: to dress up, wind wrappers and towels into robes; Ife, Joy, Bessie, in pretend fashion shows, the walk, the pose. To play as a woman, a full woman, with a purpose that tugged, such that it was easier to go out wrapped in a towel, to go out in the towel to face the house's needs – and so it will be here, after class, after the bath.

16

In previous houses it has helped to end these hours of work with movement. A walk or a dance, as in the house in Queensbury. That was one of her favourite sits, a three-bedroom townhouse with a rabbit. That house had a mirror-walled room which the owner had converted into a dance studio. There, she would connect her phone to the speakers through Bluetooth, turn the volume up and dance. Turning and turning, as it went after uni, nights out turning to find newness, the moment when the mix at any club or bar lifted. Cold, whipping bright turning and turning. And then back at home, Efia in their room: Have you lost it?

She remembers the night this routine fell apart. It was five, and then six. Wait long enough and they will be at church, she told T, who needed somewhere to crash. They'll be out. Clockwork. Every Sunday. Trust. Walking back with T who could barely walk by then. And pushing the door back to find Mother, Father, Efia standing there. The three of them. Late to church. And T. And her. Vodka tobacco perfume. So it was back out from there into the cold into movement. From then it was only a few weeks before she left for good. Out again, after the first house-share and the next. Looking back, it was meant to be, because through this she met Sammi from Cricklewood, at a bar for birthday drinks. Sammi who ran fitness classes with a friend – a personal trainer – empowering dance for women.

'You can teach an afrobeats session,' Sammi said. 'You will be great.'

And, 'I want a teacher who can dance but, like, authentically.'

At first Mercy resisted; the idea of teaching was too much.

'Not actually a dancer,' she said. 'No idea about the authentic part. Are you OK?'

She was born here, she told Sammi, a reminder. She was last in Ghana four years ago, and even then she was too self-conscious to dance properly, too aware of her own limbs, of what others might find missing about her.

But Sammi was Sammi – she convinced her to at least try. And it was fun. To stand before the mirror, as a dozen women echoed her every move. And then Sammi got the house and her passion shifted to that. The house, a gift, after her uncle passed; he said, I hope it brings you a fraction of the joy you have brought me. And this was the beauty of family, Sammi said, with a frown, as though as she said it, she was still processing it; Sammi who had won an essay competition in sixth form – a case against the nuclear family, said she had written it after finding Shulamith Firestone on Wikipedia, while reading about technology and feminism, pale face framed by that hair, that image haunted her, as she told it; she wrote that essay to free herself, to understand, but at times, sure, she admitted, like when her uncle left her the house, at times sure, she said, the trad family had its charm. Family: a circle loving on and on to flourishing. Pragmatic, she said. For now, it served. And she had decided that happiness – that love – lay in giving, and so she set the house up as a gift, no longer a HMO but a shelter, and then Sammi gave up the fitness classes and put her all into the house.

Mercy stretches her arms.

And now she is thinking about Efia. How strange it is that they shared a room for so many years. How Efia hated bathtimes when they were young. How the flat in Enfield filled with her screams, as Mother swooped down and lifted her from their games.

She feared the bath, Efia explained, years later from the bunk below. She said, in the darkness, she feared water.

Nights in their shared room had become a time of confession, then. It was an idea that came from the discovery, in their first summer in Ghana, that Father's father was a catholic. From then on, they claimed this heritage, too, with its new afterlives and in-betweens. They had new prayers to memorise, and beads to wear not as jewellery, but to bind themselves in faith; a heritage that encompassed the beautiful churches – those with coloured glass which, in sunlight, reflected all hues of life; buildings carved with stories.

'How can you be scared of water?' Mercy asked in the darkness. 'It's everywhere.'

Efia said, 'I guess that's just how I am.'

And she – big sister, role model – made it her mission to challenge this. Back then it was everything to show Efia that the world was safe. From the first time Father placed the bundle of little sister into her arms. At their cousins' house, in summer, she put on a show, for Efia, splashing in the pool. And on church trips, after the long coach ride, chasing the boys to the seafront, wading into the grey to taunt the waves and hurl stones.

But it was not the water Efia feared, it turned out, more what the water concealed. Those stranger forms, those other lives, and the motion that carried them, the way everything deep below in the water moved, how despite their depth, those other lives seemed to hover, how in water nothing alive or dead could rest, nothing held still, the shapes that filled oceans and seas and lakes. Those other beasts that ruled the black depths in silence – they were real, she had seen them, they all had. And worse than what they had seen – the thought of what they had not seen.

She feared the creatures in the documentaries that Father played often around that time. Father: no longer standing in black outside Zara, gone too from his evening shifts, nights on which he stood outside theatres in Covent Garden, with the lights, street performers; gone from that standing life – everything I do is outstanding, he used to say – gone from there into work that allowed him to sit, to pass hours in warmth, back in a vehicle. Not in a cab, driving people as in that past life in Ghana; driving a van, a large white van to collect things, although now and then he collected people, too; driving again, progress, still not quite there, so he said over dinner, back to eating at the same time, all four of them as a family ought to, he said, as we did in Ghana. This is how we did it, growing up, he said. Natural, he said, it took time to settle after a move, even across one city, how much more to another continent. It would take time, he said, to find their rhythm; he was close, heading back a familiar way, driving the van to collect parts to re-cycle, people too, and their possessions – whatever needed it – better, since, with this job, he could work as much as he pleased to save for things like this, time to eat together, and later to buy the satellite, followed by the computer, in which opened another view from the flat, a view to sit above other views before, the satellite: which marked the start, the metal dish he fitted, with his own hands, he and a friend fixed the dish like an ear outside the flat, a dish on the wall by the kitchen window, a treat, he said, and so it was: spaciousness, that new view into the world. The satellite beamed in football and documentaries. On his days off, Father sat in the glow from the TV and called them – his two daughters – to watch, to sit with him, and see more of the world. And this, he said, was why they were here – to see more. This became his answer, whenever Efia cried, whenever she said she did not want to live in Enfield, but in Cape Coast, at Grandpa's house; Efia, who wanted sun. Her own room in a bigger house. Father said he had moved to this country not to work – that mattered, sure, but he had moved, and moved them here, to see. So they did on their documentary nights. They sat to watch the real-life shows, as Mother used to call them, animal documentaries which ended in tragedy – that's real life, that is nature, that's just how it is – documentaries that covered myths, Bigfoot, the Loch Ness Monster, mysteries of deep-sea life, with the same serious narration for creatures mythic and real, and often the real ones were most horrendous on the screen and that was why Efia screamed at bathtime, and why water, in that scream, became the world.

17

It is twenty past six and she is still here, at the desk. An ache is setting in across her back. This is the result of taking too long to move. To close the lid on the laptop and walk away from the desk. To cross the study and head back out to the landing. Here, in this view, after all these hours of sitting before the screen, from here it is as though the present has blurred into the past, as though the house with all its paintings – of market scenes, sunsets – and the sculptures – figurines that hold vigil on window ledges, the faceless women in motion carved from black wood, or the ground-floor figures chiselled from deep-grey stone – as though all these pieces belong to a parallel world.

She has felt like this before, though never so heavily as today. It is a kind of strangeness that comes gradually, as a haze. This is the view that came from emptiness, that in the past grew from that gnawing inside, a view that in previous years came from that other life, a view that belongs to the weeks and months gone in the church, during which time forgot itself, that season of noise and music and prayer and emptiness, the pangs that not long ago sliced through this same gut; here in this view – intermittent as it is, this sense of time collapsing within itself – the perspective that, when it comes, in this haze, after class, this is the spiral that defined life before. This is what follows hours of eating nothing, empty, and in that: full circle; whole, the same view that, when it comes, fades the house, flat – any house – even here, so far from where it happened; in this moment, the house is translucent; the view from that life, after each fast – though it won't help to dwell on that here. To search again for a slant of truth in it, to try to salvage light from before, a different kind of knowledge, in the music, the wailing; it will not help, enough attempts have made that clear.

She has the feeling she could get lost in these memories. She has the feeling she could stay at this desk all night. So she gets up; she pushes the chair back and stands.

It is easy from here. She steps away from the desk. Out of the study, and down the stairs. She moves on slowly, keeping watch. From here, the cats might appear below in the hallway.

On the ground floor, all is quiet. Again, she moves gently, so as not to scare them if they are near.

Still, as before, there is no sound of movement. She walks on through the bedroom, and from there to the bathroom. She twists the tap and water splutters white.

She will keep the bath short tonight. Already, she has lost too much time in these memories. There will be no time for a walk tonight either, to head outside before calling the client. Tomorrow, she tells herself. For the walk on the second day of this sit helped. The walk was a way to get out of these thoughts, out of these memories. Easy, then, with the camera, and lenses in the backpack; she followed the paths to capture the forest, queer and honest as it was in the fading light, in its shadows where the light fell honey thick.

On that first walk, there were couples; she saw them from a distance.

The thought of them, on the paths, as they may be again tonight. How strange to think of them, unaware this house exists – and, for this, further away – imagining themselves alone, unobservable, spectral, less and yet more than present. In this there is at least some affirmation of this feeling, that it is not easy to be certain that this house – these rooms – exist.

18

At times Ekua is slow to answer messages. Though, on the app, she appears to be online.

Mercy sends another message, in case she missed the first.

Hey, Ekua. Are you free to chat? I'm going mad here.

19

The last time she saw the cats was on Monday, day one. Here, in this same hallway. But even then, she only saw Ubuntu.

No sight or sound of any of them since that day, even while leaving their bowls out in the hallway each night.

Every morning, all three bowls wait – empty. Which suggests that all is fine; they may still be here in the house. But thinking about it now, what if something else has been emptying the bowls?

A creature – something small – may have slipped in through a window, or come in around the back doors. A door left ajar, though she has tried to keep them closed, in part out of fear that this would happen, that the cats might run away. They were nervous even then on day one, flinching from their own shadows, and she had the feeling they might run out to the meadow. So she has taken care to keep the doors and windows closed. She has also kept the house sealed for fear of what might come in.

After all, for all its quiet, this house is surrounded by life.

★

It could be a rodent that has been eating the cats' food. These woods are filled with them, as the client said on the tour.

The rodents, she said, made her adopt the cats. As long as a few appeared, now and then, more could follow, and with the cellar incomplete, she feared they might damage the art collection she kept there. It seemed, then, she said, that the world was resurging, the world as in nature, wilderness, returning. She said that early in the lockdowns, when she still listened to the news, the story of nature itself resurging comforted her. The idea of the world, without people, growing back. But it also implied there would be more life – in all its forms. She said this convinced her that the rodent problem would only grow worse. With this in mind, she adopted her cats. This and the need for company. At the time, she was not alone in that, she knew. It was nice to feel part of a whole again – to be one of many to adopt a pet.

Once they were here and part of this house, the idea of life without them was unthinkable. She looked back on the past years as a self-inflicted punishment. Though, she said, she had not planned to stay here alone. Certainly not for so long. Said she would not have moved in had she imagined how thoroughly the world would close.

They were in the music room, on the second floor, then. The music room: the only room in the house that has a theme. All its pieces depict people swept up in dance. And in the glass cabinet by the window are flutes and drums. The client said they were crafted centuries ago. It was here that she told of how still the world felt through the lockdowns, quiet, yet restless underneath. She raised a hand and tucked a curl back under her scarf. Then something shifted in her gaze and she continued. She said at the time the idea of living here had seemed like fun, fun as in diverting, as in different – an escape; at the time the idea had represented, at least in theory, not a withdrawal, but it had seemed like it would be something of a release.

'Because it's so quiet here,' she said, 'so much itself. I thought it would be what I needed.'

'I think I get that,' Mercy said. 'You mean you wanted to have, like, a break.'

'Yes. A break. Something like that,' the client said.

She said that it helped, to begin with, the calm in here. For some weeks, staying here meant a pause from the noise of her life, though not a break from life itself – and here her brow furrowed. True, she said, on moving in here she had kept much of the world at bay, such as with the WiFi – which she limited to the first floor. The connection is for the study, where she worked for the first few months, at the desk, lecturing. Most of the house, particularly the ground floor, is offline.

Still, living here was meant to be a temporary break, and so it seemed idyllic, and more so with the necessity of protecting her health, immunocompromised as she was. It was also an experiment, to see how solitude might help after her divorce. Her life was too spacious then – and here, she laughed – too spacious, she repeated; she had never imagined that would be the case, but it was true, she felt as though her life no longer fitted. When she moved here she was still trying to fathom how to live well, alone.

Adopting the cats brought relief, and balance, she said. She said she hoped Mercy might enjoy their company too.

Mercy rests her back against the wall. Beyond the sound of her own life, the house is still.

No phut-phut of paws, no echoes of movement. In stillness the silence is heavy with more of itself.

On her phone, she sends another text to Ekua:

Hey, Ekua. Are you free to chat?

20

Back in the front room again, where she left the suitcases; even here there is no evidence that any cats live in this house. No shed hair is in sight. Through the window, a mist of rain hangs over the meadow.

She takes the cushion from the large armchair and hugs it to her chest. She is stroking the tassels on the edge when it happens. The faintest sound, from the hallway. Like paws on the wooden floor.

Still holding the cushion, she steps out to the hallway. Too quickly, perhaps. For now, looking down it, there is nothing. The space is clear, all the way to the stained glass at the end. She holds still, and listens. Nothing. She walks the length of the hallway, with the cushion under her arm. Small step after small step, so as not to scare them. At the far end, rain is drumming against the glass. The wind has picked up, too. It will get worse, the forecast said.

Back down the hallway, into the front room again. Her heart pounds in her ears. It is hard to remember the sound that drew her out just now. Let alone to think about whether it was real or imagined.

Mercy sinks into the big armchair. Across the room, the

fish in the tank are still moving back and forth. And there on the coffee table, as she left it, is the list.

She takes it up in both hands. Smooths the creases over her lap. The letters look so assured.

Dishes to cook. Friends to invite. Photos to take.

This, more than all previous houses, is perfect for hosting, ideal for a reunion. If the rain clears, they could take photos out in the meadow, or by the lake.

But to ask the client later, without her cats there on the call. She sinks back, hugging the cushion. Here in this room is the same feeling from years ago, at uni, the anticipation when she used to decorate her room for hosting. She can still remember how good it felt then, to intentionally curate a space for relaxation. And now she is thinking of Liliana, of their nights in.

There. She can still feel it: a second layer under the skin, even now, after the years that have passed. Eight or so. She remembers the night when they first met, and their walk back from the open mic night. It was freshers' week, and she was determined to experience as much of the place as she could. At the open mic night, it was a relief to slow down. She was sitting at a table at the back of the hall. A girl in a sequined shawl appeared and asked, is this seat free?

The girl offered her name, Liliana, and her hand.

In the interval: I love these rings, where are they from? And: Your accent – are you from London?

And the girl, Liliana: Yeah, in a way. But. No.

The boarding school she had just left was outside London, she said. But her dad also kept a flat in Islington. She had hoped to study in London, UCL, she said. She had applied to LSE, too.

'Always felt I'm meant to be in London,' she said.

And:

'I get this a lot. Like I'm from places I don't belong to?'

And then:

'Oh, this is me. Watch my stuff!'

She went, between tables, to the yellow of the stage. Liliana, summer eyes: pools of gold under the lights. Looking out, taking the audience in with her smile, one hand curled around the mic. Later she said she saw nothing from up there. The room dazzled.

She was overcome by how easy it had been to reach the stage, how the room had shifted to nudge her to stand there. And there, in the light, she was looking for a way back. Not to hide, but to get the book she had left on the chair. If she had gone, she later said, she feared that she would not have found the way back; it was easier to draw on memory up there, she said later, with the sense of spirit softening from bone, with the notes from the piano, and the giddiness awash in light, and from the cocktails, too many too fast, two for one at the SU bar – yes, it had worked, too well – and now there was a chance of falling on the walk back, so she stayed on stage and drew on memory.

There was a strand of something so sure in her pauses, the movement of her hands, as she leaned towards the mic.

She was not a poet, she later said, but at times words overspilled. She said the next three years were experiments in her eyes.

And after the readings, as they left. Into the chill, she said:

do you ever think
about all the lyrics you know?

She said that years earlier, in a poem, Black History Month at school, her own words had abandoned her.

Then her voice, on its return, brought words that were more than hers. She had never experienced anything like this before. All she could think of in that performance were words from other artists, lyrics from childhood songs, blues and soul – music that had formed the rhythm of her thoughts, and shaped her urge to write.

'What, were you tipsy?' Mercy asked, trying to picture it.

Liliana laughed. 'Not even,' she said. 'I mean, I was messy at school. But not that messy.'

At times, she said, I get this rush; if I'm lucky, it lasts. Then I can create; I know I can make it.

It was understandable then, she said, the way those lyrics had interrupted her. Those were the words that had made her write in the first place.

'I keep thinking,' Liliana said, 'how many lyrics, ideas, you carry, without knowing.'

'You are still in flow,' Mercy said. And they laughed.

That night they walked until Mercy's block reappeared. The tidy bricks and tinted glass. The bike stand. Subconscious, the path that led them back. Inside, the room was bare. The room had nothing to offer to anyone, besides the cereal bars in the box on the shelf. The bars were snacks, to keep herself from ordering Domino's. It was first term and, with the bursary, she was determined to save up for a camera. A serious one, good enough to travel with. It felt possible then, to reach for more; she had arrived on campus with a simple plan: to live responsibly, save up, and, by summer, buy a camera. Later would come more lenses. Then she would save for plane tickets.

So the room was empty that night, with little to offer to anyone. But with Liliana, and all they had yet to discuss, from then it felt important to make more of that space.

Those months felt good, with jasmine and lavender candles, hot chocolate sachets from freshers' fair. She bought new speakers, to play jazz. And with that came the discovery of what a space could become with effort and good company.

Liliana. In the glow of the laptop, first at the desk and then on the bed, with blankets for November: after lectures, to watch interviews with the dead. Words from poets – the living, too – Mercy had never heard of till then.

Liliana said:

If I were a lecturer, or more like when. Because no way can I hold down a regular job. When I'm a lecturer, this – she pointed her chin at the laptop, where bell hooks was paused, mid-sentence – is required reading.

Yet a difference remained, in the spaces between them. Even when there was nothing, skin to skin in the bed. The distance came in part from memories. To talk was to shine a light on spaces they had not shared. Their lives had been so different up till that point. On Facebook, clicking back, at times she looked through old photos. Liliana: boarding school, in chequered uniform.

They stayed on campus through Christmas; in those weeks she told the parents her first major lie. It was easy, with the distance, to smudge the truth. She told them she was ill, that she needed to stay to rest.

Which was true, in a way.

She was not hiding, though, as Liliana said she was.

More distance, then; Liliana's family was liberal, close.

Liliana asked, the day it snowed: What would your parents think of us?

And Mercy laughed. Could not imagine why it might be relevant. Then she realised Liliana was waiting for an answer. She sat up. The last they said directly was, well, some things you have to find out the hard way.

Liliana laughed. Her laugh was wonderful. Her laugh shook the mattress.

I like them, she said. Your parents.

Please.

They speak in riddles, Liliana said.

Peace filled that room, as they watched the day's light repaint the walls. Ease. Too much, perhaps. On New Year's Day, Liliana said she had never been so relaxed; she said that she had even stopped taking her pills.

I want to try, she said. To see.

Mercy leaned up on her arm then, to look at her. Um, what pills?

Liliana waved. Just stuff I used to take for school.

She said that now she had stopped, she could feel herself returning. She could feel a brilliance cutting through the haze. The world settling back into high definition.

'I didn't know,' Mercy said.

'What.'

'That you took anything.'

'Mercy. Everyone does. But.'

'But?'

'But that's the point. Right? You didn't know.' Liliana stretched her legs and rolled over onto her side.

'What did you take?'

'Nothing. Honestly. It's my stepmum, Lucille, being Lucille. So I ran away from school one afternoon and she lost it. Apparently she could not fathom why I hated it there. Had to be something she could pay to fix. Voila.'

Liliana said she was not close to her stepmum. Therefore, it was not fair for the woman to set her temperament. That the previous summer, she'd tried her first experiment, which she had treated as a warm-up for these three years. That just like you can curate a living space, you can curate a family.

She said, 'We were half joking, at the time, but we were serious. We name each other, what we see, what we need. I have sisters, brothers, nieces; I have a grandmother in there as well.'

She had built a whole other family in London. 'I was so sure I'd study there. I was going to stay at the flat.'

Her father's place, she said. In Islington – hers, for summer.

And she had found it, a community. Though it was unlike this, the sense of closeness, it was diffuse there. This, she said, to pass hours inside and feel complete, was new.

Then came exams. And with that season, a reminder: holding a place here relied on proving merit. Over and over, to prove a right to remain. From there it was inevitable that the balance would unravel. No more time for soft nights in – nor to wander around campus, nor, eventually, to reply to Liliana's texts. How far away she was, with her family, with the flat, and then with another gap year to follow her graduation. The year of travelling was a surprise from Liliana's father. He said she could treat it as part of her inheritance early, that it was the least she deserved for keeping herself together through these years of change. He told her this in a voice message Liliana played out loud in Mercy's room. It was there again that day, a distance between them, as it had been from the start, the awareness of how much more most of the other students had, how although they were here together, they did not share the same experience, and then the news came from London. Her own father, lifted too much into his van, heard a crack. It was nothing, the doctor said, nothing is broken, it is just the nerves, but Father said he had heard it, he felt it, something was broken. She saw it clearly then: Father, his wiry frame, holding up their world; Efia, Mother – and how frivolous this place seemed. And from then distance became necessary, a kindness.

But then the first exam, for all her worry, was easy, fine; on walking out, to Lili's. To say, sorry; I lost perspective. She stood by the doors. Dialled, waited.

Days later, lying on the bed in her room, a call shook her phone. And:

Hi, this is Lucille. Liliana's guardian. Is this Mercy?
Hi, she said, sitting up. Hi. Yeah. This is. This is Mercy.
Hi Mercy.
Hello.
Hi. I'm calling – so, I think you two were close?
Yeah. Um. Is she with you? Mercy said.

Yes, she's here. We're at home.

Warmth rinsed through her. Can I talk to her? she said.

This isn't a good time, actually. I was just calling to say, well, we're fine.

A pause.

I don't know if Lili said, but she gets manic now and then. She's all right, but she's had a low. You'll understand we need some space.

Later, an email:

> She's locked everything else down. This is Lili by the way. Yeah, I'm okayish. Hope you are too? I think I was just doing too much. What can I say. But. I believed, you know? For a while? Well. Doubt I will be back. If I am, not soon. Maybe I'll reapply to a London uni, heh? Maybe I'll quit trying to learn anything, full stop. Maybe I'm lost because you know, even now, I don't think the issue is how I feel. This world? Should I be well adjusted to this? Does it seem sane to be happy in this? The planet is dying. Most of the world is living in need. And we do what, write beautiful poems about it? Anyway, it is what it is. I think I romanticised us a lot, to be honest. I will miss you. I hope you get your camera soon.

From then on, the videos YouTube suggested were all Lili. Echoes of her. And the girls, the girls were a world away, in summer internships; the group chat was all pictures from offices above London.

Mercy bought the camera early, second-hand, from eBay. Took it in her hands one night and walked.

21

The phone lights up with a new message – finally.

Ekua.

She leans back against the wall, relieved.

> *Mercy, my lovely. How's it going? How are the fish? I love watching fish – so soothing. I've just seen your message – in a meeting but will call soon. xxx*

And below, a missed call. Another missed call from Mother. Which suggests that the first call – earlier – was not a mistake.

Something like dread seeps between her ribs.

They have spoken about this before, she and Ekua. Ekua said it is more common than she had thought. For daughters to struggle to reconnect with their mothers.

'It's something I wish we could speak about more directly,' Ekua said. 'Because it's a thing, a conversation, something I had to work through, too. But it's worth it, because you know they love us underneath; their intentions are all love, just it gets distorted, you know, in translation. I felt like I had only just started to feel properly in sync with my mum before she passed,' Ekua said. 'So I'm always going to encourage you to reach out, Merce. To set things straight, keep things open. It's easier, I think, when you have some distance, you know? And maybe that's when they start to see you as your own woman.'

It would be easy to tap the screen and call back now. Just like that – to open that door again, to see what – if anything – has changed since their last call. But. The last time they spoke did not go well. The last time was Christmas. She was sitting a house in Bermondsey, for a couple who had travelled back to Devon for the week. They had wanted someone to watch their two Dalmatians while they were away, and had stocked the fridge with Christmas-themed meals in neat portions. They had said they liked the idea of opening their home at this time of year. And when Mother called one night, to speak on video, in excitement Mercy showed her the decorations in the front room. She showed her the tree. And Mother said she was living as though she had no family of her own, as though they had not given up so much for her.

Better not to make the call tonight, she thinks now. Best to wait till after the client says it's fine to have company. Better that than to sit alone after a call that will likely end in tears. And for the call, it will be safest to have something to offer to Mother. Something beautiful to focus on – a view, or a photo. Another lake, perhaps, for Mother's collection.

A memory: a lake. And a village. Home before all other homes.

Another memory: turning the pages, cross-legged on the rug, with the leather-bound photo album across her lap; in plastic wallets: faces, smiles, eyes; and later, looking for more, with the camera – the big one, from Father's desk, the one with multiple lenses to screw on, the camera Father said not to touch – wait for the click before raising it to see.

Mother first told her about the lake in answer to a question she brought from school. The question:

Where are you from; where are you really from?

She remembers how that day, she wanted to settle it for good, find an answer that was more than Ghana, the flag; she wanted a place more specific –

Mum, (yes?) where am I from

that day in the kitchen, and:

Mum, (yes, my dear) where are you from

She was sitting in the corner, swinging her legs off the stack of chairs, with the taste of corned beef salty-sweet on her tongue, the pinch of corner meat cold from the can: a prize for staying near while Mother cooked, and after a pause Mother said: where are we from, oh – you know. You know the lake.

In photos, the lake: sun-burnished. Gold. A question: is it real (of course, you can see it, can't you) and (that was when. We used to go. Oh. Your father took that picture).

The lake: body of rain. Receptacle. The rain that filled the lake was not the reason for its shape. This lake: a gift, Mother said, drawn by a deity's hand.

This is the story Mother will tell this Saturday. She will tell it at the school she runs with a group of friends, where she teaches on heritage. The class that, on the phone these coming days, she will ask Mercy to help her teach.

Mother will say this is the vision she started from. That she had hoped the two of them, and later Efia, could teach together. To teach the class, on Saturdays, is to give back. She will say there is still space for a prodigal to return, that freedom, love, success, brilliance mean nothing without this, that all is vanity without a return; without giving back in this way. She will say it is a privilege to be able to consider this, a blessing to be well and safe enough to bless others. She will say, when they speak, that life falls through different seasons; a mark of growth, of womanhood, of flourishing – is in this. That a sign of growth is in returning to give, to sow ahead, to cultivate beyond the self; she will say this stage of life, the three of them: here, well and grown, fleeting as this will be, mother, Efia, Mercy, complete, present – that this is supposed to be the time for bearing fruit. She will say, in this season, giving back has to come first, and yes, it will cost, yes, there will always be more to think about beyond this work, there will always be a reason why the present is not enough, but she will say that it is not elsewhere God has called them to worry for, that rather all their striving has led to here.

A plea, an invitation, will follow then – a request to return together. Not just back to London, and the room they rent in that church, not just to return by closing the distance physically, but to travel back to an earlier time, to wind back to that summer, to its simplicity. The first job: teaching, a real job as, yes, it paid, though not very much, sure, but it paid, Saturdays, in the room, the building theirs for a time, there Mother will likely tell the story of the lake – of home.

Father will disagree, with his smile, which though suppressed still finds a way to show itself. It is ironic, he will say – to tell that story about souls and deities in a church.

And then an argument will follow, but only the playful type.

The memory makes her smile. These arguments mark the outlines of who they are, the borders of their shifting perspectives. These are the differences underneath that push and pull. If Father mentions it, the next time they meet in that building, if he comments once again on the irony of telling that story there, in a church, Mother will laugh and say, no. It is not that strange. It is possible for different truths to hold their space. A story can make sense from different directions at the same time. And if anything, it makes more sense, to remember it there, in church. And the church is not a church anyway on Saturdays, she will add, that room which held that closeness that seemed spiritual, heightened – where two or three are gathered, as they often said.

A building will be all that its occupants ask of it, and that building is not a church while it is theirs; in memories, and in their Twi and Ga lessons.

They will unroll the posters – the maps and language charts, something of home for those who have yet to go back, though they will travel back, too – and at the thought, a smile tugs her mouth – the date, as ever, is soon: they will see the places they have glimpsed from that room, in photos, including Bosomtwe.

*

Mother said the souls of the dead pass through that lake. And for their family, the lake is where their love began. Mother says the lake brought Father into her life.

He drove into her village to take tourists to see the water; he: a driver – and more, as he said, in the following weeks, in the time of explaining themselves to each other. Driving, he said, was not his true calling: he was the latest in a line of carpenters, a line that reached back to the first tree and the first man. Time on the road was not his destination, but it served, and even then, in that car, as a driver, he was more. That day, he was also a guide. A translator, too. And for a fee – he became a photographer.

This is where their family began. Father says the first sight of his future was through the lens; when he pointed his camera at the lake – the woman in the corner of the frame, with her head bowed. He found himself arrested by her stillness, could only watch, held by the soft lines of her arms, how they flowed up to her shoulders, to her neck. When she appeared, he took the photo at once. This image, poorly centred, tilted, he says is the best photo he ever took. He kept it, the view from which their love began, the view from which more love has since followed. Two wonderful daughters. He kept that photo as proof of their beginning.

Though Mother will say it did not start like that. She saw him before he noticed her. From his car, sputtering close, the same vehicle that later took them out on drives, though at the time, she said, and laughed, she could not have imagined enjoying that. Driving – whether the motion, the smell or both – troubled her; she said this later when Mercy complained about it, too, as she sat with both arms crossed over her stomach on the drive through Enfield to church.

So when he climbed out, unfolded his height from the

seat and stood, arms akimbo, the sight of him beside his cab troubled her. At the time it was his presence that bothered her, his alertness, him with a group of foreigners waiting in the cab, soon to climb out and map themselves against the lake, turn their gazes to the water and sky, and have children to run to them with open hands. He was complicit, she said later, in a betrayal she could not name. Still, it was there, an urgency between them.

She cried when he asked her to travel abroad with him.

He said they would return. If they could leave, they could surely return.

She said her life was there, by the lake.

He said his eyes were tired; he had seen every road in Ghana twice.

Still, she said, for her, life was there. Home was the place that drew more of itself closer. Her relatives were there, and the constellation of her friends. Childhood on that shore, dunking each other into the water, hands meeting in darkness, to pull each other up.

She said she had known this would happen since he arrived. From his restlessness, and his atmosphere. The way he existed on the brink of perpetual motion, in part from his hours on the road in his music. All the cassettes he later brought to London in a backpack; she can still hear the clatter falling over the floor. Father's cassettes: a soundtrack to the beginning – in Enfield. Later, he would tell of the places he drove through to that sound, memories interwoven with the rhythm of the past. And the photo – he framed a copy and hung it on the wall in the flat: Bosomtwe. From there, they hung views of more lakes around it.

During the first week in London, Mother said, they

found another lake. And then another and another, more bodies of water than a city of this scale deserved. In undulating fields, where the water was busy with ducks and geese, they took a bag of bread on days off from working in shifts. Then, to return, waterside, to stillness.

22

When they speak, Mother will ask about the course.

The question: When will it come, the time to go back and graduate.

And this is the official reason why her place at home is gone.

A memory: a photo, on campus by the lake. The four of them. And in their smiles – a promise.

At times the idea of returning does make sense. That it might be possible, worthwhile even.

It was only meant to be a break.

Time off for grief, the university staff said, in an office that smelled like Dettol.

It was understandable, given how terribly the first year had gone.

After Liliana dropped out, the ache of missing her; after it eased enough to sit through lectures again – him. The other person it seemed important to host in her room. Him, with the laugh. Green eyes and that smile, curving up and up. He was intrigued by her, he said. He lived in the next block. She used to see him at the supermarket. At the library. By the bike stand. He said he was curious to see how alike their kitchens were. And their rooms. If they were all the same. Like prison blocks, he said. She was curious about him, too, then. She wanted to know what he would say if she invited him over. She did not have to let him stay, though. Not for as long as he did. She did not have to invite him back over the following weeks. Self-inflicted chaos, she later said, back with the girls at Bessie's, in Ponders End. Together trying to make sense of that year apart.

The girls had faced challenges, too. Bessie was in the middle of a crisis of belief. Time away from her home church had made her question her faith. She had lost weight. She said she was too anxious to use the kitchen when other people were around. But next year would be better. She had found a studio to rent alone, so there was that. But she had received so many rejections lately, she said, rejection after rejection while applying for internships. Only a relative of a coursemate had found her a placement that summer.

'I don't know what is happening,' she said.

Ife said she had felt it, too. A distance. To be surrounded by students who had been told all their lives they were the best. Who spoke with certainty, even – especially – when they were wrong. 'But regardless, we're here,' Ife said. 'We still made it. We're good.'

And that was when Mercy told them she was not good. She told them then about the heaviness of her year. That with all the loss, she had no plans to go back.

'Look. I fell in love and she left and then I met this guy.'

Him, with the smile. And. The rumours from other girls (not from her) and from his gap year: alleged harassment in Magaluf. The incident on campus – which it will not help to dwell on now – reasonable, the staff had said, to take time off.

The staff seemed grateful that she had not replied to the journalist who got in touch. As though her silence was a choice, and not a force of its own. They said the issue was not just on that campus, it was as serious – if not worse – elsewhere. Unwarranted – dishonest – to reduce it for a story. Grateful, and with that, her place remained. Take your time, they said, come back when you're ready.

It was Joy who cheered her on the most through those weeks. Joy, who of the four of them had survived that first year intact. Said she was planning – dreaming – to take a year out as well. She wanted to travel, to practise Spanish and volunteer. She said she was tired of looking with envy at those on her course who had already done so. Sure, others had had the means to do it earlier – to travel, teaching and planting trees – sure, they had already done it but the chance was open to her as well now. She wanted real life experience, she said. Joy, who, more than the rest of them, had known from early what she wanted, if not the details of how to make it happen. She had set her heart on aid work in primary school, said she could not forget her grandfather's village, the Easter they flew back. She wanted to build new houses, with better plumbing, indoor toilets, power, and with time she said she wanted to run her own development agency, and later she decided it should be an exchange for the diaspora. She was on the right path, she felt, and she wanted experience, to make it feel real. With a year out, they could travel together, she suggested. Mercy could go ahead, and they could meet up in Ghana. It was exciting, she said. She could take her nature photos there.

'So proud of you,' she said. 'Can't wait to see the real world!'

And though it never happened, though London drew them in and held them fast, through those months, the possibility helped.

Still, at times, such as now, the idea of returning to finish the course, properly, glimmers. To go back first to move on – to finish – to graduate.

It might be illuminating, to study now. To understand more of how the world works or does not in black and white. And in this, to clear a path. To start again.

At times the idea of returning seems possible. And then there is the debt, ever growing.

23

Back to the bathroom, again to the sound of water. Back to Bosomtwe. And so it goes, as it was in years before. To imagine the present away – mind from body – until the lake. Not as it is in Mother's stories – of origins, of where-you-are-from – not the lake as it was there but as it was in her own return, the lake as it appeared when, after years of planning, it turned real, ice against skin. And the funeral. Mother's old church filled with mourners, in black and white, the sermon, liquid in Twi, unbroken, no English words, and no pauses through which to ask and enter the meaning. It was the funeral of Mother's auntie's friend, though Mother had never mentioned this woman until then, had said nothing of the woman who had raised her after Nana passed. Dust to dust, water to water. At the lake, she put on a show for Efia, who was eleven then, Efia in her jellies, sitting nervous on the shore. How easily the words came, knowing Efia needed them. To say: Only water. Offering a foot, then a leg – to the blue.

The lake, Father said then, was a wonder, that much was sure, though not because of souls or gods as Mother said.

He was a man of science, he said, that day in his black and white. Though. He had left university early, too. An argument (futile) on returning (Dad, you did the same), back at the flat. On dropping out. He said, yes, he had left, but not in the same way. He said he had enjoyed it, studying had opened his world. Not least because he had chosen what he called a sensible field, a practical field, earth sciences, although it was true he was no expert upon leaving. He might have become one, had he stayed to finish the course. He said that he had left to work for his siblings' school fees, three brothers and one sister all born after him; nonetheless, he had learned enough to read more for himself and later to watch, to see for himself, as they did with their documentaries.

These thoughts – unclear how they help. Yet these are the memories that overflow in this quiet. These are the memories that have been suppressed for too long. It was hard, in past sits, in London, to face these thoughts, given what followed: an undertow. There were not enough years between the present and the worst. In London, while close, Father, Mother and Efia in the same city, easy, then, in theory, to close the distance, so much that it did not matter, at least in theory, on leaving, nineteen, end of summer, packing the suitcase, leaving, Merce, hello? where are you going? Efia in the hallway, um, hey, what's going on? with the suitcases, and the backpack, into the lift, down and out and on, and then up onto the bus, and after the journey: the first house-share, and the next, the next, and then Tottenham, and then Sammi's, in Cricklewood, the haven, the relief of the kitchen, the way sunlight poured in and filled the sink on clear days, flooded in and met the tiles – a shade of teal that made the room watery – and how the fragrance of fresh linen suffused the house, and the washing machines, three in the side room never stopped, so the house seemed to tremble all day, and the smell of the fridge – white vinegar, from the efforts of a woman who feared that roaches would return, although she said she had not seen them here yet, but they had shown up in every shelter she had stayed in before, and at times it took weeks but they came, they followed her, so the smell – vinegar – chilled the air each time the fridge opened, a reminder – in this house were women who had survived worse, who were rebuilding from and with less, Cricklewood: the interlude, where she became useful, again, cooking, with the pans full of light soup, recipes that were too big to cook alone, even there, with the uncertainty of whether Sammi might want to try, mutual admiration, before they settled into friendship, a love that outgrew the initial shape of desire, admiration, respect that fed the urge to do and give, and when the line around home softened, when Mother called and said, we are still here; which was to say there was still room in the flat, at least in theory, there was still room to return, although by then it was clear that the room would not be the same, the room would be new with her absence, and with Efia's absence, too, by then; and anyway a return would not mean forgiveness, but rather going back would mean compromise for them all; the line was only soft as Efia had left for uni, the room was quiet – the line around it gone. So it was possible in London to return. Mother said, we are here; but, have respect – if you come back, don't bring your foolishness.

And:

God is testing you. It will pass. This cannot define you.

But she is not there, not now, but here, with the bath.

Heat is rising in waves and fogging the room.

She types the pin into her phone and unlocks it.

Still nothing new from Ekua. So, she decides, she may as well use the bath.

There is a calm that only comes here, in the water. Partly, it comes here, in these last steps before. It is in the routine of getting ready, securing the room, with the anticipation of the sweetness that is to come. She steps into the water and sinks into it. Luxurious, it felt, the first time, to have a whole bath, and with that, to have so much time to use it. To wash, with no pressure. No housemates waiting to use the loo. There have been beautiful tubs as well, baths that cried out to be filled. She rests her head back and closes her eyes. She thinks of Efia again, what she might be doing now. Whether she ever got over her fear of water. Whether she really feared water at all. A laugh bubbles through her. At times it seemed that she played it up to make it her thing. She wonders whether Efia would answer if she called her number today. If she would still ask if Mercy knows she can come home. What she would think of her plans to leave the UK. Of starting a new life, over and over.

Losing track of time while bathing feels reasonable at least. Better than standing around caught up in memories. This is progress in some way: to refresh, to ease up here. Had Gemz been here, she would have called it wasteful. It was inefficient, she used to say, to sit in dirty water and allow your skin to wrinkle up. They were staying at a hotel once, when Gemz complained about bathing. Mercy had bought incense – a new set – as a surprise. She had bought oils, too, from Camden Market, for massages. It was funny, how at first Gemz resisted, and then, with time, slipped into enjoying it.

Gemz could be anywhere tonight. She always said she needed to learn to slow down more. Her childhood home was busy, she said, no time to waste on baths. There was always someone else waiting to use the shower. A bath? she said then, appalled. Then they laughed.

It is hard tonight, though, even here, to come unstuck from these thoughts. And perhaps with good reason. There is more to do. For one, she ought to get out of the water and look for the cats properly.

She feels better with the bath done, her body flushed and warm, here, in leaving, unbolting the door, the click; and now, on pushing the door back to leave, in the pause, a habit, from previous houses: to wait on the threshold, and search the stillness for a sound, for movement, a creak – a footfall – from the house, and when, as happens, nothing comes, to step out.

Back through the room, carpet like silk under bare feet, out from the steam, from the hum of the fan, to the door, and once here, at the threshold, by the door to the hallway, this too has become a habit: to look back through the haze – the steam, where sweetness clouds the room – back to the blur of mirror above the sink, and through the doorway, with the day having closed around itself. Now there is time, it is nice to reset the lights for the evening.

It helps, the client said on the tour. During the pandemic, she bought these lights. And it helped, while alone through those months. To adjust the colourscape. Bluetooth controls, bulbs in various tints. She bought them on an impulse, she said, nostalgic for when it was nothing to pile into friends' living rooms, when they lived close enough to fill each other's houses – not here, though, she said, they have yet to warm this house.

And this, she said, helps in the quiet. Softens the dark. After the bath, with the lamp, its neck of gold.

Now it feels open, this room. This space, somehow all hers, and hers in a way that few other spaces have been, in a way that reaches for the start, for no one else has slept inside this room.

The only time like this was at university, another room where no one else had slept before, the room, dreamless; in this, a new room in the new block – a first choice within another first choice, as though it were true: as though desire alone was enough to bend the world. Satisfaction, even when that hope came to nothing, after its collapse, the memory: what it was to stand in scenes from the prospectus, first-choice university, and then first choice of halls; first the choice of where to live, and the first chance to really live.

There it seemed that existence might be enough – this was the place all previous places pointed towards. Yet it was not a conclusion – it felt more like a start: a look at what a place – her place – could be.

She was in the newest block – unreal, in the pictures: single bed, the haze from the window – a virtual illustration, as though the room was yet to be built, but it was there, on arriving, that first day on campus: after years of hope, not just hers, the whole family's, for she was the first of their line to study in the UK. We have Arrived, Father said. A whole en suite, clean fittings, opening the cupboards and pulling drawers out, running the tap until steam billowed, and later, after photos, parents and Efia on their way back, later, while alone, she climbed onto the mattress, stood on the bed and looked out, and considered the months to unfold around this space. People to meet. Ideas soon to line the shelves. The room, new and hers, so she told the girls later, when she called: a promise, to speak regularly on the phone, as they had seen their mothers do, the girls in their parallel beginnings, in their new rooms. For a while – for the first weeks – so it went, emailing photos from their cities, and then came the urge to decorate that room to reflect, to soothe the ache, from the absence: of Mother's voice, Efia's complaints, Father's whistling; from then, she went out to poster sales, garden centres, charity shops to look for pieces with hints of who she might become, for these were the years, as Father had said, on the drive, with the van choked with boxes. This is the start, he had said – in this, a plea: don't mess this up; which meant: don't do something you will regret.

24

Ekua calls here in the bathroom, when she has just finished scrubbing the bath. She is wiping the mirror to smooth the fog away. She almost misses the call when it comes – the phone flashing, noiselessly. She scoops it up and taps the screen just in time.

'Hello?' she says. She puts it on speaker and sets it down on the towel, on the edge of the bath. 'Hello? Ekua?'

For a moment there is nothing and then at last:

'Hello.' Ekua's voice sounds tinny from the speaker. 'Hello?' she says again.

The sound echoes off the clean bathroom tiles. The screen flashes again with a series of beeps. A request to switch to video.

'Are you OK?' Ekua says. 'Are you good? Hello?'

Mercy says, yes, one sec – just finished cleaning the bathroom.

'Super,' Ekua says. And from there, her voice falters, fragmenting the rest. She is saying something about conditions. Or no. The conditioner. She's asking about the conditioner.

Mercy wipes her hands on the towel. Her fingers are

crinkled. They smell of detergent mixed with the lavender bath bomb. 'I haven't washed my hair here yet.'

The conditioner is still in a suitcase. A sample made by a woman in the housesitters' group chat. Ekua suggested weeks earlier that they might get on.

'I think you would enjoy documenting your hair journey,' Ekua said then. She was evangelical at that time about making video content; it was, she said, a beautiful means for self-expression. 'It's especially important,' she said, 'if it's beyond your comfort zone. The most natural way to connect. Talking. Face on show. It would be sweet, ironic, if the internet brings us full circle, no?' And, she said, for someone in Mercy's situation, with debt, it is worth considering how a viral moment could help. 'Besides, it seems like your challenges are at least partly from the hit your confidence took. With the church. And your break-up. If you start a channel, to share – authentically, I mean, and you will – with that, you can take your power back. You already teach, you know, same deal. And this matters, right, how to care for our hair.'

'I'll try it soon,' Mercy says now. 'I'll defo try it when I get to my hair. It's just been baths for now. This place has handmade soaps.'

'Ei,' Ekua says, 'I bet it smells so good.'

She says more, too, but distortion blurs the rest.

'One sec,' Mercy says. 'Wait. I'll call you back.'

Days like these are reminders that this closeness is tentative, despite how real it feels. That for all their conversations these past months, they have never met in person. Someday they might. For now, these virtual check-ins must be enough.

The signal improves a little way down the hall. Still it is patchy, here on the ground floor. The rain is back, pattering overhead. The signal is still too weak for a tour, not strong enough to show Ekua through the house as she had hoped.

It is stronger – enough to call back – on the stairs. On the screen, pixels settle and Ekua's face appears.

It is morning in San Mateo; her face is backlit by amber sky. The wind has thrown her sisterlocks across her face. She smiles, and smooths her hair from her eyes.

'So,' she says, 'I just had the longest meeting. About the house – in Koforidua.'

This brings a smile, and a memory: Ekua's drawing from weeks ago, a photo of a page – a disappearing message.

A house, one of an innumerable sequence of similar plans, including her own – fantasy houses in Ghana. In this case, the house was Gemz's idea, too. Gemz said it would be fun to have a place back home, as in a place that's ours, properly? She said that was the biggest shock from her summer in Ghana, the first time she went back with her family. She said she was surprised to see how vast the houses were, how much room there was in and around those buildings to run, she and her cousins and their friends chasing a ball, sneaking up on the lizards and chickens. She said then that a supply teacher had once told her that they were lucky, here, she and her friend from St Lucia, as they sat there at the front of the classroom, working. They were fortunate, the teacher said, to grow up in the UK, with a view of the best of both these worlds. At the time, Gemz had said, as she recounted this, those words had angered her, as she and her friend sat at the front, writing in their books, at the front and at the top, sure, that was true, but cornered into that place; a sense, she said, that, in her teens, bore her deeper into herself. Gemz said that this was while she was still figuring out how to exist, how to settle in the spaces where there was no music to cover the rough edges, no noise in which to hide her attention, stop her mind from noticing more of what bothered her, so she was angry then, she said, though she did not yet see it as that, knew it then only as hurt, another shade of loneliness, but she was angry then, at the teacher's presumptuousness, at the idea of this gap in which she found herself: born here, yes, but not of here, and when back home – when in Ghana – too, still not close to enough; outside, then, everywhere, in between on either side. She was annoyed that day by the teacher's presumptuousness, the idea that this gap was more of an opening than a void, that the teacher could not see abundance might involve dissonance, that what appeared as everything did not mean completion, that excellence came from need as much as it was an overflow. She said that was before she found a way to stand in that place, to root herself in the shifting of that place, to alchemise that initial fury into sound, to make it hers, which was to make music of it, she said. Nothing new at the start; she was putting melodies together. It was in the sequencing, lining up, overlapping. It was in making that she discovered there was more room, more than enough room in the sound for every shade of light in her chest – but there, Gemz again, pulling at these memories, these thoughts circling around a different house. This conversation is about Ekua's house, a meeting just now, as she said, about that house, her new project, about the place in Koforidua.

'Yeah, how's it going?' Mercy says now. She tries to remember Ekua's latest update about the house. 'How was the meeting just now?' she asks. 'Are they actually building anything yet?'

But even as Ekua answers, it is hard to focus on her words. Her mind still reaches back for that other house. How good it felt, just to imagine together. At Gemz's place, after dinner, sketching boxes on a page. How easy it was to mark the lines, walls and partitions, and then to shade areas outside for growing. Cocoa. Shea. Oranges.

'I remember how the oranges in Ghana were so green,' Gemz said one evening. They were sitting at the table after dinner, too full to move. Sleepy, comfortable, in the mood for daydreaming. The sun was soon to set; it was autumn and the daylight was fading. It was easy to lose track of time there, too, with a good meal, with the light dimming. Gemz had been saying how much she missed the light in Ghana. From there they had got on to imagining having a base there in the sun. 'And they were so sweet,' Gemz continued, still on the oranges. 'I remember feeling like my whole life had been a lie.'

Gemz said later, as they moved the plates to the sink, that she knew a group of musicians who had moved to Accra. They had moved back from New York for the Year of Return, she said.

Mercy asked if she had met them in Ghana.

'Not even,' Gemz said. She pushed her sleeves up and turned the tap on. 'Well, not yet. I just liked their stuff on Soundcloud. So I reached out, like: Yo. Can we chat? This fusion group, like, jazz and highlife, with a dubstep twist. And we got talking. They live in Accra. People are doing it,' she said. 'They are.'

Those were the happiest times. Dreaming back for the same home. To travel Ghana – making music, images. There was a time when Mercy daydreamed about it so much that, at night, the house came back in dreams. As though it existed already, waiting for them.

'You get?' Ekua says, startling her back to the present.

Back to here, on the stairs. In Meadowlight.

'Yeah,' she says. 'For sure, true, true.'

'And this is just to buy the land. Can you imagine?' On the screen, Ekua glances back across the stretch of road. Behind her, only a few cars are in sight. A grassy verge rises, bleached yellow. And then the sky, luminous above. 'But how are you?' Ekua says. 'How are you liking the house?'

She had intended to focus this call on the cats. To explain the situation – that all three have disappeared. That they have been hiding since she arrived. She had meant to ask how to find pets that do not want to be found. But instead, what comes out is a description of the house. Not of the building; it is the quiet she describes, the sense, through these past days, of falling out of time, and then the awareness of the heritage in here. How memories keep resurfacing in the stillness.

'I had a place like that,' Ekua says, after a pause. Her eyes are bright, in the frame on the phone screen. 'Ages ago. Some places are so quiet they send you into yourself.'

'Yeah,' Mercy says. 'That's exactly how I've felt.'

She laughs; there is relief in this. Perhaps she is not losing her grip on reality, then.

'But in a positive way,' Ekua continues. 'I don't know. How are you finding it?'

'Good, I think.'

As disorientating as it has been, the quiet has been kind.

And it has been a relief, to have this space to look back. To think through moments she has not recalled in years. 'It's been good. Not what I expected, I can't lie, but if this is to be my last house in the country, yeah, it's great. It's different.'

'Your first country place.'

'That's true. There is nothing for ages here.' She can feel it now, how far the rest of the world is from here.

'First of anything is strange. Be patient with it, yeah?'

'Yeah,' she says, and shuts her eyes. 'This is the thing. I may have been too patient.'

Ekua laughs. 'Please. Is that a thing?'

An idea comes to her, as she sits with her eyes closed. 'Wait,' she says. 'One moment.'

'Why, what's happening?'

'Wait, wait. Just one second.'

Mercy leans back against the step behind her. The edge presses her back and, after a moment, the pressure is soothing. Here, holding still, with the darkness behind her eyelids, it is possible to hear the house again. Soothing, this, as it was when she was a child, to sit and just listen to the building like this. A way, looking back, to settle to sleep. A blessing, Mother used to say then, of living in a busy city. To hear its life, its restlessness beneath the quiet. The world goes on, she would say; no matter what you are feeling, the world is still there. People are laughing, others are walking from place to place, others are playing and eating food. 'Did you hear that?' Mother would say as they held still. 'Listen.'

And they listened together, on the sofas, or on the rug. To the thuds and clicks and stomps from the homes below theirs. Muffled conversations, the murmur of radios and TVs.

Now, as she listens, there is only the rain, with its static fall. And it is OK. The silence feels spacious now. Perhaps because now there is someone to share it with in some way. It will be better yet, she thinks, if the girls visit soon.

'You still there?' comes Ekua's voice. 'Hello?'

'Yeah,' Mercy says. She sits up and rubs her eyes. She stretches her arms, and looks over the stairs again, down to the hallway. 'I just needed a moment. Hey. It's just hitting me how much I may have messed up.'

And it is. The house is huge. The house is wonderful. But.

'How can I lose three grown cats in four days?'

On the screen, Ekua smiles as though she's suppressing a laugh. 'Sorry, sorry,' she says, and laughs. A musical sound. 'Cats exist to troll us.'

Mercy sits forward and hugs her shins.

'Either way, this is a chance to see how you get on with houses like this. You will get more,' Ekua says, 'as long as your review is sound enough. Quiet houses. And you can travel! It starts from here.'

'Yeah.' Mercy places the phone beside her on the step. An idea occurs: instead of looking for the cats, it may be best to stay up here and watch. With enough time, if they are here, the cats are sure to come out. Better yet, she could set a camera up here. She could set it up to record the hallway.

'Ekua,' she says, 'when I first saw the photos of this place.'

'Yeah?'

'When I first saw it, I thought it would be.'

'Let me guess. Simple?'

Mercy laughs. 'No. Not even that.'

'What?'

'Romantic?'

Ekua laughs. 'Ooh. That reminds me. So, can you have guests?'

She says the plan is to ask the client about that, tonight. They will speak soon, and she can ask about inviting the girls. 'I don't know, though,' she says. 'Feels awkward, if I have lost the cats.'

'Have you not told her?'

Mercy shakes her head. 'We are meant to speak in, like, an hour? I don't know. I might find them by then. I need to just look. Properly. I haven't yet. I lost track of time, and then I kept getting distracted, thinking back. And to be honest, this house. I don't think I can properly search this place alone.'

'Still ask,' Ekua says, 'but tell her first. About the cats. Because who knows, maybe they have run away before.'

'They haven't,' Mercy says. 'Otherwise she would have said.'

'You should still say,' Ekua says.

'Yeah. Just I haven't looked properly. If I still can't find them later, I'll set cameras up. There is no point mentioning it while I have barely even looked. This place has so many rooms they could be anywhere. I need help, for real.'

'Which you'll get, with company. As long as your friends can visit.'

'Exactly.'

'You're fine. And with this sit. Even just on the app, you'll see a new tier of houses. And you'll get more responses. I'm so excited for you!'

A thrill tickles her spine.

'So. What's she like, the client?' Ekua says. 'How's the distance?'

She tells Ekua the distance here is strange. The client talks about herself a lot.

'Her email this afternoon was literally an essay. But it's

mainly about her work. There are no photos of her family or her life.'

'And the other way? Does she ask about you?' Ekua says. 'I remember, you were worried that people would ask about that church?'

'Yeah, no, she doesn't ask. Actually, I think she has her own idea of who I am. She said I reminded her of her grandmother.'

On the phone screen, Ekua frowns. 'Her grandmother?'

'Yeah. Exactly.'

'Oh, hold up. Wait. Where is she from?'

'The client?'

'Yeah. I heard countryside house and I had a picture in my mind.'

'Her grandmother was from Benin.'

'Benin. Oh. No way.'

'She showed me a photo. And the thing is, I sort of see it – dark skin, cheekbones. But, I mean, this was just one photo. Plus it was black and white.'

'Ah.'

'But it can be more than appearance that brings someone to mind, right. She told me her grandmother, from Benin, married a man from Algeria? They were both involved in independence movements.'

'Interesting.'

'So they marry, then have her father in Benin? Son grows up in those circles – this is her father – exiled to Paris, in the sixties? Moves to London and marries an Irish woman – her mum. They have her in London. So she has this Pan-African heritage she is super into. She was telling me all these exiled friends of her dad would visit them when she was growing up. She has a book in her for sure.'

'Sounds like it.'

'And she has written one. Like, a textbook, I think. But her personal life – her family – sounds like a lot. She told it like she was conflicted about it?'

'Yeah?'

'I guess it's weird, because I'm in her house. I don't know. There was something off about how she said it.'

Ekua is quiet for a while. From her silence comes the rush of traffic.

'Does she have kids?' Ekua asks.

'I don't think so. I didn't ask.'

'Sounds like she's absorbed with her work.'

'Yeah. I've been pretty caught up in my own memories here, though. I just want to feel like everything these past years, that it doesn't add up to nothing? I want something I can look at and say, yeah, I am here. I am something, you know? I've been thinking a lot about these past few years. I was even thinking about starting a channel the other day.'

Ekua beams. 'Ei. So you are considering it,' she says.

'Just reflecting. So much has happened. I honestly just want to have something to show for it. So much has just slipped through my fingers.'

'I hear that,' Ekua says. 'After this house, you will have so many options, Mercy. Freedom.'

'This is the perfect house for reflecting as well. Wish I could show you.'

Colours blur over the screen, before they settle into focus. Ekua: walking again. 'What, no tour?'

'The internet is patchy. The rain. Thinking I might take pictures in the rain. I had this idea for a shoot. A second Garden of Eden.'

'Is this for photos of the pets?'

'Not even. My friends from Enfield?'

'Yeah?'

'Yeah, so if they come, we can make portraits here. We used to dress up, do our hair, and then we would go out into someone's garden or the park for photo shoots. We made all these pictures through the years. If they come and it's still like this, we can just try and take photos in the rain.'

'Can't you take pictures inside, with the art?'

'No, no pictures of the art.'

'Ah,' Ekua says. 'What's it like, though? All African?'

'Yeah, from all over. I've seen pieces from Morocco, South Africa, Botswana. Modern stuff and old. It's nice.'

'But?'

'Did I say but?'

'I heard it.'

'Okay. It's nice, but it was more how she said it: No pictures of the art. This was after I sent my portfolio and offered to take photos.'

'You sent your portfolio? Ei. Look at you!'

Mercy smiles. 'At this point I have no shame. And it would have been fun, to shoot here. She said she wants to open this place as a retreat. But about the photos. You know what people said, back in the day, about cameras and souls?'

'Yeah. Why?'

'She said something like that, too. That taking photos of art can degrade it.'

'What?'

'Yeah. From what she was saying, she lost her job in academia. Maybe she was— But see. None of this is my business.'

'Yeah,' Ekua says. 'Keep it profesh. Keep it simple. Especially if she said you look like her grandma. What is that?'

'Yeah. Okay. I'm gonna eat before the call.' She looks down the corridor towards the light that is spilling in from the kitchen. 'But. Yeah, I'll ask about having company. Wish me luck.'

'It's raining, you said?'

'Oh. Yeah.'

'They'll come home. Your cats will come back in no time. '

'I didn't even think of that.' Mercy opens her arms and stretches again. 'Honestly,' she says, 'thank you so much.'

'Pleasure.' On the screen, Ekua smiles.

Her thoughts spin back, to the church, before. Tottenham. Gemz, in her room, by the window, against the grey, and the relief, the spaciousness of those first housesits.

'Really, everything will be fine. The girls will come – we'll make beautiful photos. I'll call my mum. I want to sort things – I look back and it's so scattered. I was thinking about this earlier. And when I say this, allow me.'

'Nonsense! Non-sense!' Ekua says.

'Allow me!'

'Madame.'

'Ekua.'

'I know what you are going to say. We were having a nice conversation.'

'Listen.'

'A year of quality coaching and you come back saying what.'

'Ekua. You know you said you're here to listen?'

On the line, Ekua's laughter bubbles.

'I appreciate it. Our conversations. You know, you need to learn to accept compliments.'

'Noted.'

‘Thank you. For real,’ she says.

‘Merce, thank you,’ Ekua says. ‘It’s nothing, honestly. This is it. Someday, you can mentor another, and we pass it on and on and on. Anyway. Don’t stress. Enjoy it.’

25

In the kitchen, the sun has set, and the windows are black.

She takes a plate from the cupboard. Removes the leftovers from the top shelf in the fridge. Rice. Spring onion, egg and soy sauce. Though the fragrance is dull, and the aroma less urgent than it was before, the flavour still calls time back to the past. Wood Green, with Auntie E, when she was well enough to cook, her cane resting against the cooker. Even to step, when the radio broke into music.

Before the church.

Mercy places the cats' bowls on the counter. She refills each with a helping of dry food. Best to take them to the study for the call. The cats may still show up in time. They may emerge during the call, if they hear their owner's voice. One final look over the kitchen, this empty room, and then she takes the bowls, and her own meal, up the stairs.

26

The line opens, as it did previously, with a hiss.

In this there is relief. For perhaps the line will be fragile again tonight. If it is bad enough, they may have to speak some other time. By then the cats may have returned by themselves. By then this cold feeling in her stomach might be gone.

'Hello?' the client says.

Static gushes around the word.

'Hello?' Another pause. And then again, under more noise. 'Hello. Can you hear me?'

Mercy says, yes. She can hear. And: 'Shall we switch to video?'

Her hands tremble as she opens a browser on the screen. Then, all at once, it happens: the call connects. Her face fills the screen, a reflection, flipped over. Then the client's face appears, too, a blur of beige pixels. She is wearing glasses today, squarish lenses, with dark frames.

'Oh dear,' she says, and the rest of the sound crumbles to fizz.

The client is sitting by a window, in a glare of light. Her

face sharpens into focus as she moves nearer to the camera. Her hair is up, wrapped in a deep-green scarf, its darkness splashed with orange fragments or birds. Orange earrings swing past her jaw.

'Oh dear. Sorry,' she says. 'Yes, this is from my side, I think. I'm so sorry. Ah, there you are. That's much better. Hello?'

'Hello?' Mercy says. The word sounds flat. She clears her throat and tries again. 'Hello. Hi. Can you hear me?'

On the screen, the client's eyes are glazed, distant.

'Hello?' she says again, this time louder.

Mercy glances back to the study's open door. No sign of them: Oyo, Ubuntu or Sankofa.

On the screen, the client waves. 'Hi, Mercy. Are you there?'

'Yes,' she says, with the feeling she is not.

Instead, she is elsewhere, in a slow-motion fall. She feels as though she is sinking towards a hard truth. A negative review is sure to follow this, one that may be severe enough to end all previous reviews. Bad news stands out, blood on a page. People react. Addictive, it can be, to indulge in schadenfreude. It is built into the business models of most platforms. But, she reminds herself, there may still be hope for a way out. She sits up and folds her arms on the desk. Ekua has said that she is building up a reserve group of clients, people she has worked with in the past who may be willing to take a chance to help those stuck with poor reviews. There may be people who can offer sits for those who are trying to improve, for sitters who need to boost their ratings. Ekua said she is working on it, but it's hard with bad reviews, she said, especially if the cause for the dip in a sitter's rating is reasonable. Some clients leave bad reviews with unclear grounds. It is easier then to move on and land more sits, but when something definite and measurable has gone wrong, such as damage to property, or neglect of pets, when something has clearly gone wrong, it is hard to secure more sits.

Mercy presses her palms together under the desk. She clears her throat. 'How about you?' she says. 'Can you still hear me?'

On the screen, the client's face softens.

'Yes. Here we are,' she says. 'Good to see you.' Her smile broadens and she leans back. 'You look well,' she says. 'I'm so sorry about the connection.'

'It's fine. It happens,' Mercy says, her voice even, pleasant. 'Yeah. It's been good so far. The connection, I mean.'

This much is true. She tells the client about the maths class she taught earlier. How smoothly it went. How much the students enjoyed it.

'Wonderful,' the client says. 'Well, let's keep this brief. I am sure you have more important things to do. How are you? How are you finding the house?'

'Yeah, great, thank you,' Mercy says. 'I'm enjoying it.'

She turns the volume on the laptop speaker up. Tenuous, sure, but there is still a chance that the cats, if close, may hear. And no one is near to complain about the noise.

On the screen the client is squinting. There is a slant to her eyebrows.

'How about you?' Mercy asks. 'Did they find your luggage?'

It is easier than she had expected, how conversation moves away. The client says that sadly the suitcase is still lost.

'But. I am writing a new speech,' she says.

'Amazing,' Mercy says. And it is. The client looks relieved.

'It is still early,' she says. 'But the words just came. And. There is something about writing it out a second time.'

She says that exploring helped, that she went out for a walk – a dérive – with the city's pulse under her shoes.

She leans back and blurs again. 'Where are my babies?'

With this, the air hangs still.

'Are they around?' the client says. 'I'm sure Sankofa misses me. Poor thing. Is Ubuntu there? They're not sleeping now, are they?'

Mercy wipes her palms on her lap under the desk. Ekua's words echo inside her head. It is best to tell, and sooner rather than later. But. This is different. It is still early. She is still new in this house. And the client will only worry if she hears the truth. Her first time away from the house in years. She will panic if she hears the cats are missing, and it will likely be for no reason. The house is vast, with enough hiding places for them still to be somewhere inside. It is not as though she has really looked for the cats yet. Even if she had managed to stay focused, to look properly earlier, if she had not put it off, lost in the memories that resurfaced, even if she had looked, there is no way to search this house properly alone. She will need help; it will be easier with company.

'Yeah. They're OK,' she says. 'They're downstairs.'

Once the words are out, more words follow. And now she is talking about how quiet the cats have been through these past days.

'They were downstairs, the last I saw,' she says. 'They've not come up here much, as in here, to the study, and it's hard to do a video call downstairs,' she says. 'The WiFi. Especially now that it's raining again.'

'Yes,' the client says. 'Oh. Poor things. They are probably wondering where I've gone! Well. Have you taken any portraits so far?'

For this, too, an answer flows quickly. No, not yet. She will take photos later on.

'I tend to take pictures of pets a few more days into a stay,' she says, 'to get a sense of their personalities. Hmm. Maybe I'll start next week. Should be sunnier; it's better with more light. But I'll let you know. I'll send a few once they're ready.'

'Ah. Brilliant.' The client's eyes shimmer with her smile.

It is not dishonest to blur the truth like this, she tells herself. This is part of the role: to reassure, to let the client enjoy peace of mind while they are away. Sometimes a little creativity is warranted.

'I think the cats need time to get comfortable with me,' she says. 'Pets can usually tell if I'm still settling in.'

'I'm sure,' the client says. 'The quiet takes getting used to.'

She says she has left wine – in a crate in the kitchen.

'I meant to show you, when you came up for the tour. A friend left it. I find it helps when it's too quiet. Some nights. Oh. Do you drink?'

Mercy says, 'Yeah. Now and then.'

'She's just taken over her family vineyard,' the client says. 'My friend. A lovely family. They were friends of my father, maybe I said, in his exile. Lovely people. Oh. You speak French, Mercy, don't you?'

Mercy nods. French: she had forgotten about this. The flag that she had added months ago on the app. Temporary. She had added it as an experiment to see whether two languages might attract more replies. Sure, she is not fluent, but she has studied French before. With Gemz, when they were dreaming of travelling Francophone Africa. Gemz's idea. From listening to a friend's mix. She said she kept thinking about how strange it was that those countries felt opaque. Togo, Ivory Coast, Burkina Faso – seemed closed away, despite their proximity to Ghana.

'Have you been?' the client asks. 'To Bordeaux?'

'No,' she says. 'But. It's on my list.'

'You have to go,' the client says, smiling, 'it's heaven in summer.'

'Does she have pets?' Mercy hears herself say. 'Your friend? If she ever needs help.'

The client laughs. 'She will love you. Anyway, please help yourself to wine. And let me know what you think of it. My friend asked for reviews. Oh. And the cooking. Tell me, please. How has that been?'

Mercy sits back in the chair. This at least is comfortable terrain. 'Yeah,' she says. 'It's been nice, so far. I need to pick up more shopping soon. I was thinking it would be good, you know, to cook for people here.'

She mentions the meals she would like to try soon, the recipes that it would be a shame to try alone.

'Did your mother teach you to cook?' the client asks.

'No, actually,' Mercy says. 'I learned from an auntie.'

And now she is explaining about Auntie E's catering business. It feels natural, sharing this. There is something real in the client's eyes here on the screen. She remembers the rule about keeping a distance, maintaining professional boundaries with clients, but here it seems that perhaps the rule is more of a guideline. So she goes on talking about cooking with Auntie E. Memories from the roadside kiosk her auntie started in Ghana, first in Accra, and then later the chop bar she opened in Cape Coast. How, while in

London, they used to go together from church to church, with an envelope of leaflets, working through back-to-back functions, the superwomen team, Auntie E used to call them, cooking with Auntie E's friends. They served in kitchens at birthday parties, reunions and funerals, at engagement parties and graduation dos.

'I actually got into taking pictures first to help promote her business,' she says. 'My dad had a camera. Then I got into taking pictures of the events themselves.'

She presses her fingertips against her cheek. Too long has passed since these memories resurfaced. Too long has passed since she found the space to unfold them. These are good memories, too, despite the ache that follows them, pleasant memories from the time when every church she stepped into felt like a new home. The discovery at that time of an endless community of Ghanaians, of believers, worshippers, with familiar songs and stories and hopes.

'How lovely,' the client says.

'Yeah,' she says. 'I always felt at home in new churches. It was even magical then, in a way, like, how you could prepare something that made people feel at home. Everyone enjoying, just dancing, moving. Anyway,' she says. 'I would love to have people over. To cook for some friends here properly, if that's OK?'

The client smiles. 'Oh, that sounds wonderful,' she says. 'Of course. Please do. That sounds lovely.'

PART TWO:

The Girls

27

She feels the change even before she leaves the bed.

On the phone, she looks again at the map she shared in the chat the night before: the hours of green around the house, and then on stroking up, south and south until London: the knot all the grey lines tangle to.

Now, underneath it, the chat is all gifs. As it went in years before. When it seemed as if real life happened here, in their hands.

Perhaps she slept so soon after sending it, hoping for this. Hoping for a dream to unfold, as the client warned could happen. That dreams in this house can be startling with their clarity, night visions. Perhaps this is an effect from an artefact below, as the client suggested, during the tour. Perhaps this came from an ancient piece locked in the basement.

She dreamed about one of their sleepovers. This time, the four of them were staying at Ife's place: the maisonette by the chip shop, the side of the parade where the air hung slow with grease, vinegar perfume, where they used to stand and hug farewell when morning came. They had claimed the living room, with their nest of quilts spread over the floor. When blackness soaked the room, and warmth shimmered around them, those sleepovers felt as though they had slipped through the centre of the night, and as though the truth of light – of vision – was in darkness.

This house would have been ideal for sleepovers. With all its rooms, its spaciousness. But the client said last night that while guests are fine, no one else could stay at this house overnight.

Now Mercy thinks of those sleepovers with the girls, for holidays, birthdays, Halloween, Valentine's Day. Ife's mother said it was important to mark holidays then. Ife's mother, in gold jewellery.

Ife's mother said it was important for them, as girls, and more, as women-to-be, as Africans, the mothers of the mothers of the world. She said that holidays would help them to mark the passage of time in good company. A holiday, she said, should reflect its observers. Just because their peers were using them for sin or laziness did not mean they should miss out. It was, she said, their right as children of the Most High, their purpose, as a minimum, not to miss out on joy in this life.

A memory resurfaces, with the dream still palpable: a sleepover that they held to mark a birthday. Her seventeenth. It was to be their last sleepover before adulthood, so they booked a suite, in a hotel, for the first time, their first sleepover in a home of their own making. Home, then, was any place the four of them claimed as such. A thousand homes-to-be existed, waiting, and so it was natural, then, to believe adulthood would unfold in the same way; that the future would be about finding more spaces in which they could be themselves. The memory: with Ife, Joy and

Bessie after school, relinquishing her bag – shrugging free of its heaviness and following the girls out through the gates and up onto the bus.

Bessie had booked a suite on the ninth floor of a hotel. The room was high enough to see across London, to look out, with her arms wide. Lights awakened, as darkness fell, and the view glittered. The room was high enough to see outside for miles, and yet not so high as to make the city appear abstract. The room: still low enough to keep the street below real. She remembers the heat that clouded her stomach on leaning out, how sparks skittered through her arms as she pointed her camera out to the dark. The suite, its perspective: more real than school earlier had been. And the contrast, from school to here, enhanced the shine. School, by then, was a place to go through the motions, to look and act as though they were learning, when in truth there was small hope of that happening there. For it was impossible to change, or grow, when rigid, afraid; not that school was scary, but they knew by then that it was no place for ease. They knew which teachers looked for reasons to punish them, which girls were most likely to spread gossip about their homes, so the first attempt at what has helped through housesitting, the first attempt at tutoring, came from doing this with the girls, teaching each other after school, from evenings helping each other with their homework on MSN: the relief – logging on at the time they had agreed earlier at lunch, to work together and prepare for the next day; Bessie's mother's idea, that between them was enough wisdom to solve any problem.

Bessie's mother: in Ghana, for her national service, had taught at a secondary school in Kumasi, and now she worked for the council, answering calls, but she was still a teacher at heart, she often said, and so it was she who suggested that the girls study together. And it was fun – to meet again on MSN. Ife even typed up agendas, emailed out lists of items for them to address as a group, and, with that, school became a hollow place – a performance; only upon leaving did the world turn real again.

They had all stayed in hotels several times before, but they had never been together in a hotel that was at once so far from and yet still close to home. Before, hotels had been for holidays, overseas, and, with that, usually with family, sharing beds, and they came with pressure to go out and return spent; hotels in years before had been places to shower and sleep in, and then to leave; they were not destinations, they were not staying places. That evening the hotel was an experience in its own right: room service and the screen and the speakers: karaoke, an institution for Ife, who already sang with her church band by then.

It was easy, then, to show up for each other. To live out the sisterhood of their mothers' prayers. She can still see Mother, as she was all those years ago, from the times when, in prayer, she, Mercy, opened her eyes, when she looked – to check, she would say, to make sure Efia was not peeking. Often she was, and when caught Efia said she was trying to see if Mercy was looking, and often their eyes met, and they tried to swallow their giggles, and Father's hand around hers tightened, a squeeze that said, focus, have respect; we are in the presence of the Most High. Still at times she looked, again to Mother's face, her calm, and marvelled: how a face closed off in prayer could be so open, in those days when they prayed every night, before dinner, in gratitude, returning, and Father would say, this is our time, to remember who and why we are. And when Mother's turn came, she prayed for them and the girls, the girls who meet our daughters when they leave this home, she said, and perhaps she mentioned the girls because meeting boys was forbidden then, boys will come later, as the parents often said; so it was girls who had the power to shape them, in these years, these important years, the foundations of their character, so Mother presented them in prayers, for God to sift; sift them, Father, she said, thoroughly, please, and let them know goodness within themselves, let them shine and bless one another with your grace and love. Let them form bonds to edify one another.

Your friends will show you and the world who you are, Mother said. Be careful, o. The devil has many masks. Wherever you go, please remember that. Your friends will polish the best of who you are. And it was true, in a way, for with the girls she grew honest.

More so that night, the seventeenth, saying it.

There had to be a moment to look back to as the start. It was clear by then that as an adult it would be important to show up, that she would have to be honest about the shape of love that felt true. If she had learned anything from church it was this: ask, seek and knock. If you don't claim it, your blessing, if you don't ask, it won't find you. And still even then, the truth came out first in a game – as they were playing truth or dare. The words had been gathering in her chest since forever – a relief, then, saying it, here, aloud, saying it and not typing it in the Facebook chat, which had replaced their MSN nights by then. Not saying it at school in the library, but rather here, saying it here in celebration, here in this space, all of it theirs for the night. To say the words and sit with them was to accept, to stop wondering if and then how a desire so vast and insistent could be a trick. And it was obvious, though a surprise – on saying it – that they knew, of course the girls did. They even knew about her first crush, Kara, from dance after school.

'So obvious,' Bessie said. 'And you always go quiet when we chat about boys.'

'Yeah. And your face when my mum was saying about that petition,' Ife said, narrowing her eyes. At the mention of this, heat prickled up Mercy's neck. She knew at once what Ife was referring to. She was talking about the debate that had been shadowing their churches all year, about whether marriage was only supposed to be about men and women. 'She knows, I think,' Ife said then. 'She said she had a friend. Ages ago, who disappeared. Apparently she was into women, too. So I think she is just sad, because the friend – she just vanished. They were close. They knew each other in school.'

'Don't disappear,' Joy said.

'Yeah. If anything happens,' Ife said. 'We talk first. Promise? Don't just go. No matter what.'

She said, of course. Besides, where would she go?

28

The girls – who are now women, as Joy reminds them, in a paragraph that explains how cringe it is, that she gets the ick whenever she hears anyone refer to women as girls, at which point Ife changes the name of their WhatsApp group to that, Girlies Chat – the girls agree to visit on the bank holiday.

In the morning, before they arrive, Mercy bakes a crumble. The kitchen warms with the fragrance of berries. She stands by the door as the crust turns gold in the oven. In the week since she sent the house's location to the girls' chat, the place has changed again. For one, the cleaner has visited, and now everywhere but the kitchen smells of vinegar. The windows here stand open, too, as the cleaner left them, with a chastisement.

'If you cook, open the windows,' she said. 'Not the fan! The windows.'

The cleaner: petite, with a wispy presence, dark skin and fine features. She could have been anywhere between forty and sixty. From Somalia, she said, having let herself in with her own key. The memory of the encounter – though brief – still brings warmth, the relief of seeing another person. Mercy had hoped to talk about the house, about the client, and how far this house is from everything, but the cleaner moved on down the hallway. And with her went the hope of asking about the cats. The cleaner would have spent enough time here to have an idea as to where they might have gone. If she noticed their absence, she showed no alarm. Said nothing about the lack of hair on the floor or the stillness of the house. On leaving, she only said, 'Windows open when you cook, please!'

The house is different, too, since the groceries arrived. They arrived in a van, two days earlier. She had thought to call the cab driver from day one to get a lift to the supermarket. The idea had seemed healthy, to be around people again. Alas, that day, the rain would not stop. With that, Ekua's words kept circling in her mind. That the rain may chase the cats back to the house, if they have gone, if they have run away. So, she ordered online, had the groceries delivered instead, and now, once again, the house is full.

The fridge's shelves brim with lettuce and tomatoes, cucumber, avocado, berries and cream. Carrots and eggs and oat milk and sweet potatoes. More. All that is missing is plantain, which she has asked Ife to bring. The pans are out on the worktop, clean.

She takes a photo with her phone. Sends it to the girls with:

I'll cook for you if you help me find these cats haha.

They have never marked a holiday like this, never out of London – and never in a house like this. It is their first time meeting in years, and with so much to discuss.

Even this particular holiday they have never marked. Through school, a bank holiday was just a day off for more work. These breaks only became significant with Gemz. These days were sacred in jobs from which they meant release, when Gemz worked at the cafe in Willesden Green, and she at the gallery in the gift shop. A bank holiday then was a reason to book time off from work and take a train to explore somewhere new. This memory is pleasant, not the cold shock that has come before, the heaviness in these past days when thoughts led her back. Wondering what Gemz would have made of a house like this, how naturally the cats would have settled with her here. And the stillness. She would have loved it. Gemz – who used to say that paradise was in quiet. Which was wild for a DJ to say, she had replied at the time, although, as Gemz said, music, in a way, is a form of quiet, too.

And it made sense on visiting the flat where Gemz grew up. Edmonton, in summer, when they went back for an old record. Gemz had moved her collection out of storage to save on costs, and this was an original, she said, a gift from her cousin Solomon. He passed on, she said, when they were in their teens.

We didn't see.

Gemz said he had struggled with his thoughts for years.

'The thing that gets me,' she said, 'is that we couldn't even listen to him.'

She said she suspected he had suffered with OCD; that no one took him seriously when he tried to explain how he felt. Gemz said that even she had made light of it back then. They all did. It was like a joke: there's a strangeness in this family, they used to say. The strangeness narrowed his life. His routines and rituals.

He was sixteen, she said, just two years older than her. He got it. He said he loved music because it had loved him first. Musicians, living and past, had poured their passion into the sound. It was a gift; you could tap in, inundate yourself with it. He had come over to hang out here, from his parents' house, often. Her mother told her that he had it tough back at home, so whenever he showed up, they welcomed him. She said his parents had struggled with their own difficulties; that despite how it appeared, it was not that they did not love him; it was more that they had no space to express it; his dad: trapped in a rage since he had lost his job. He was accused of stealing from the office where he had worked as a technician for years. They were tough, her mother said; Solomon was their only child.

It's mad, Gemz said, that day as they sat in her room. It was the first time Mercy had seen her cry. Tears shone on her cheeks and she did not move to wipe them away. She said she had first understood from his passing – numb at the time, beyond feeling – there had to be something to hold onto from the loss. She had decided it would be this: to look at themselves and each other, with patience, to look and see themselves, their parents, each other, as complex. She saw it clearly then, she said, that their parents were still people, still figuring it out.

Solomon loved music so much, she said again. Laughed. God, he loved it. And Mercy thought of shifting close, to take her hand. And she might have – to hold her, draw her close. But there was something fragile in the stillness between them. So instead she looked up, at the bare walls.

I mean, this was it, Gemz said, her voice small. This is where I started. Everything. The music. Started from here. And for real, I was a proper housecat in here, before.

Mercy laughed at this. What? You? No way.

Gemz nudged her and said, honestly, this is why I'm not even playing when I say uni changed everything. It was only then, really, that I started connecting with more people. She said it was easy before to spend all her time in this room. That she used to sit in the music with Solomon here and talk. They used to talk through travel plans, because he got it, too, even then; they both wanted to go. He talked about his dream to visit New Orleans someday, to hear jazz in the streets. He was saving up. He was going to rent a van and travel the States. Long term, I'll hundred per cent just move out there, he said. He sat here every Sunday evening in his records, and later the smell of weed perfumed his clothes when he returned from his walks. He could sit for hours here, lost in music, and she wondered now and then whether it had been enough, whether it had ever felt close to the freedom he had sought.

He had practically lived here by the end. Often, he slept over on the couch in the living room. Their family was sprawling. It was their strength, in a way, she said. Their family was exhaustion, gone full circle into movement. That held them close, she said, movement shifting the pressure; also, no matter what was happening, they always made time to dance. So, the beginning, Gemz said, of everything was here. Back then she used to record tracks over cassettes, and then onto CDs, downloading files on the computer at the library, then from her iPod and later with her phone, shifting the room, while her family stepped and spun and flaunted their movement, their aliveness: which became the pinnacle of every week, those Saturday afternoons, when cousins arrived, and settled to do each others' hair, to heaven each other up for church, and there was room in all the homes between them, to hold each other safe for a while.

Music, she said, in its way, was quiet, too.

'Because it covers you,' she said. 'Like, it holds you, if it's good?' She slipped the record from its sleeve. 'I made a home in it here,' she said, as they leaned close, on the bunk.

She remembers thinking about what it would be, then, what it would mean and take to return this; a bus ride to Enfield. It would not take long to introduce Gemz to her childhood home as well, to Mother and Efia, but properly, not as a friend or muse – my muse, she had told Efia, and the memory brings a smile now. My muse, she had said, when Efia found the photo, the one portrait Gemz had allowed her to post online, in Epping Forest, all its tranquillity theirs. Epping Forest, Gemz's outdoor set, and she with the camera: for promo, Operation Capture the Vibe. As always, Gemz grew restless before the lens, a few shots, and yeah, that's enough, yeah, another time. There was a vulnerability in standing before a lens, she said, she had forgotten about that part, a closeness that at times proved overwhelming. She promised to make time for a shoot some other day. I promise. One day I will. I want to. Just not right now. Yet that one photo, on her page, had Efia messaging to ask. She wanted to know who the girl with the dreadlocks was, the presence about her, the potency of her gaze. Efia wanted to know where she was from, what did she do. She's my muse, Mercy said. She holds the music together. And thinking of it then, in Gemz's room on her bed, that afternoon, thinking of what it might be, what it might take, to host at home in return, to sit like this, in the flat, and tell her half of this story, of the life that was burgeoning around them.

In the end, there was no time to suggest it – Gemz just left. She walked out from the room in Tottenham with no warning, no explanation.

Looking back from here, she suspects the asymmetry between them contributed. The imbalance, for most of their time happened on Gemz's side, in her spaces. They usually hung out at the studios she rented. There was something passive in it, visiting but rarely welcoming Gemz back to her place. She could have tried harder, she could have pushed harder to make space for them. Looking back now, it was not dissimilar to what Liliana had said before. In those months indoors, at university. That there was something like shame in how it went. To hide the time you spent with someone was to limit them, and with that to also limit the possibility of what you could share, of what could grow between two lives; to hide was to raise a boundary. But even with this, more thoughts flare up in defence. Gemz did the same, even then at their closest. Gemz held parts of herself away, too.

Even in the closeness that day in Edmonton, on the verge of more honesty, still it was there. She felt it, taut, between them – a line – a barrier neither of them could cross. Though it seemed as though Gemz was trying to at the time.

'At the start,' she said, 'I was using music like quiet, here; like a shield, honestly, I was just using it to wall out noise in here.'

She said that certain sounds bothered her here when she was small. There was more, Mercy felt it, but she never explained it beyond that. Still it mattered enough to resurface at other times, something unspeakable she had sculpted her life around. Something that had prompted her to move out – like Mercy – fast, as soon as she had another place; she too had moved out after one year of university; she moved to Brighton, the Dreamland, she said, to stay with a friend on the marina. Unlike Mercy, she had stayed and completed the full three years, although, she said, it was not about the course itself. Anthropology was interesting, sure, but she figured she could read about it on her own time. She went to university in the first place to network, she said. She was desperate by then to meet new people, people who would see her as the person she was determined to become, not as the girl she had been while living here, she said; the city compressed her, she felt smaller, restricted here. For growth, a flourishing, she needed movement, she said, she needed more space. Most of the world was not like London; most of the world was open, and less rushed. She was startled by the variety of the world, so she applied to university to meet people from everywhere. I want to travel, Merce, she said, in my dream life, I can travel, play intimate sets, outdoors, I think, like, play with sounds that reflect more than London? I want to honour the sound of this moment here as well, but I want to trace it back, like, right through to the roots? Like, I want to get underneath, everything that's trickled here to make our sound, like, underneath dubstep. Grime. The foundations. The shape of it. I want to see underneath, to play with the foundations. And it was why, back in London, post graduation, on moving out from her childhood home, she insisted on renting those terrible studio flats. Beds-in-kitchens, as Mercy used to call them, through the nights when they sat up trawling through Rightmove, beds-in-kitchens with closet-like shower rooms. Gemz cared nothing for size, she said. It made no difference. She just wanted quiet. She wanted space.

Bank holidays opened space for deeper quiet. And with that, they helped to restore balance between them. Instead of always crashing at Gemz's place, in whatever studio she was renting then, they could stay overnight in a hotel and share a quiet that was equally theirs.

The thought is there, and, in some way, it always was. Gemz would have liked this place; she would have enjoyed a house like this. And the park. Not just for the quiet – she would appreciate it as a potential venue if she still plays her forest sets.

Looking back through the glass to the garden – there: across the scattering of raindrops, sunlight glitters. She can imagine, with this view, lights hung outside, warming a path through the garden, lights glowing up towards the gap in the bushes and beyond, to the park.

The oven timer beeps. Its cry is shrill and insistent. Juice is bubbling purple through the crumble's surface.

One bank holiday, their last together before Gemz left, they flew north to Inverness. The plan was simple – to explore, take in the views by the water and, while there, to photograph the loch. She had heard that it was the deepest natural lake in the UK – it was not, it turned out, the tour guide said, on the boat, but it was the largest lake, and the second deepest. Still, it was ideal then, to add to the collection back in the flat. Back then it seemed that rituals like this would help, that collecting photos for the family would soften the rupture that split home from the present. And Gemz got it. She understood. It was a start, she said. An opening.

'I had a moment when my perspective on that side of things just flipped,' she said. They were back in the hotel room, after hours out taking photos of the light on the water. They were cosy again, sprawled together across the bed. 'I was thinking back on everything,' Gemz said. 'That was my first Christmas back at my mum's after Brighton – it went by so quick, honestly, it went like that' – she raised her arm and snapped her fingers. 'So there I was back at the flat. And I realised, maybe underneath, my parents don't, like, maybe they don't hate the person I'm becoming.' Gemz stretched her legs, pointing her toes. 'It was like, when I moved back, there was this wariness. I guess Mumz had realised that my staying there, in the flat, with the fam, was not certain. I think that was when she clocked that I would go where there was room. But yeah, I noticed it then. This wariness. They're worried, sure, because let's be real, my mum, Mumz' – she chuckled – 'Mumz is too real. Can't wait for you to meet her when she's back from Ghana. So Mumz told me straight up women are killed for this and less back home, Merce. I mean, from then, I realised most of this comes from fear. For real, and that's something I think it's possible to counter, but.' She rolled over and lay on her back. 'When you think about it, families are so random. Enter the world in this mix of characters, whew. I mean, it's not by force, but.' Her voice softened, as she continued. 'Sometimes it hits me and it's just so. Urf. But yeah. I think that showing up, like, for all I am, and letting them see in real time that it does not mean what they feared it would, that we're in a different era, a different place, all of that helps. It's important. I think it has to be. This is how we return. No?'

'Return,' Mercy said. She closed her eyes. Exhaustion was

clouding the quiet, warmth closing in. But the drowsiness between them was pleasant. And it was rare for Gemz to say so much by then. Her long reflections had all but stopped. She used to talk to herself like this to think things out, she said. And to practise languages, she monologued aloud. She said she did it to push herself to translate thoughts as they came, first into Spanish, then Twi and later French.

So now she was back, her words overspilling. It seemed like a sign that this time away would help, that it could be enough to reset them.

The following day, they took a bus across to Skye. The day was gentle, a tender light poured across the hours. They took a bus tour around the island, and when evening fell, they stayed in a cottage that looked out over the sea. The guide told them the northern lights appeared at times; they waited up in hope.

But that was then. Today is for this house, and for the girls.

29

After four years apart, the reunion was always going to begin like this, with a recap. A look back at all they have missed of each others' lives. It is natural, then, for the girls to ask about Gemz. This is why she has been reflecting so much lately, Mercy tells herself, why she has been gathering those memories into sense.

She had hoped the girls' arrival might help to distract her from these thoughts. But Ife asks about Gemz before she has even removed her coat.

The girls have only met Gemz once before, when Ife brought Joy and Bessie to Gemz's set in Epping Forest. They gave no warning, only called to say they had arrived. And they had, glittered and masked.

'We didn't actually think we would come,' Ife said then, as they hugged. Stepping back, she looked around as though she still could not believe that she was there.

'You look amaze,' Mercy said – and they did.

The whole setting was dazzling. Each moment that night, in beating colour, looked iconic. A series of perfect shots in quick succession. She was working, as she had said she would be when she'd invited them. This was her first paid gig, and she had free tickets – although, she had also said, she totally got that it might not be their thing. Yet they came.

Most of the night happened in flashes through the lens, and soon her thighs ached from squatting to get treetops in the frame.

That night the girls said they wanted to meet Gemz.

'Are you trying to hide us, or?' Bessie said.

And she was, partly. She still loved them but they were real in ways that jarred back then, in ways that seemed impossible to reconcile. And it was early with Gemz; they were still trying to figure out what they could become.

'Is she here?' Ife asks now, as they hug.

She stands back to look at them, the three of them. Together. The girls. Here.

Ife is the same; if anything, she looks more like herself. Here she is in her classic shades of cream and caramel. Cheekbones contoured, her eyebrows drawn in heavier. She has brought more stuff, she says, to glam up for photos later.

Bessie says she has brought a case of scarves and extra fits, too. She comes for a hug next, her round face – those dimpled cheeks – framed in a lace-front wig.

'It's a protective style,' she says, noticing Mercy's surprise. 'Don't gimme that look, Merce; you know I'm still natural. Don't judge me, o.'

Ife laughs. 'Wow. Bessie.'

'Hey. I'm not judging,' Mercy says through her smile. 'It suits you. You look good.'

And Joy – still wiping her boots on the mat. Joy is different. It is the glasses that are new. The lenses are round now, set in thicker frames. There is a new solemnity about

Joy. It is the way she moves as well. She seems less jumpy, smoother here.

They hug, folding each other close.

'It smells so good in here,' Joy says, stepping back. Behind her, Ife and Bessie are nodding their agreement. 'Honestly, babe. So hyped.' She lets out a squeak and looks down the hallway. 'Is Gemz around?'

'Oh,' Ife says. 'She's not doing a set, is she? Here. In the park?'

'Is she?' Bessie says. 'Ei. Look at you! That's huge. So what's the deal? Are you taking pictures for this?'

'Wait, so are we taking photos outside? Is this for the festival?' Ife says.

'No, no,' Mercy says, and waves for them to slow down. 'No, no, guys, allow me. This has nothing to do with Gemz.'

She says it then, closes her eyes and just says it. That it is over. They broke up. Ages ago. She tells the girls that they broke up about a year and a half ago.

When she opens her eyes, all three of them look appalled.

'You are joking,' Bessie says. 'Right?'

Mercy shakes her head.

'Merce. Stoppit,' Bessie says. 'You can't joke about stuff like that.'

'I don't think she's joking,' Joy says. She peers at Mercy over the lenses of her glasses.

'What?' Ife says. 'No.'

'We did,' Mercy says. 'Ages ago. I think she blocked me on socials, too.'

They all still look as though they are waiting for the punchline.

Ife breaks the silence. She opens her arms for another hug. 'Babe,' she says.

To her surprise, anger flares in her chest. Her chest feels thorny here in Ife's embrace. With this tenderness. Anger. Frustration, because this is too much – and too late. This is how it should have happened. After Gemz left, she should have reached for this. She should have reached for the girls and returned to the warmth of their promises. They would have talked it out. They would have held her. Like this.

Now her legs tremble as she steps back.

'Aw, Merce,' Joy says. 'This is a lot. We need to unpack this, yeah? Because you and Gemz? You two were—'

'Yeah,' Bessie says. 'We defo need to. But what, sorry, I'm still confused. So let me get this straight. You mean it's just you here?'

'It's just me,' Mercy says. 'Well, it's us now.'

Bessie says that from the location, from the map in the group chat, she thought this reunion was going to be about Gemz as well. 'Full disclosure, when I saw it my first thought was, hmm, this looks like a really nice venue for a wedding.'

The four of them laugh at this. Their voices echo in the hallway.

'Meanwhile,' Mercy says, 'I'm trying to choose the cat life, but even the cats said no.'

'Ei. You're serious, then. What is happening,' Joy says. 'Actually, can we pause first?' She slips her backpack off. The backpack is huge. It looks like a traveller's bag. Like she could live out of that bag for a week. 'I brought drinks. Let me at least unpack them first.'

'Eii,' Ife says.

'Remember how we used to take holidays so seriously?' Bessie says.

'I was thinking about that,' Ife says. 'You know, I used to mark our sleepovers on the calendar at home.'

Bessie reveals a bouquet of white tulips.

'I couldn't come empty-handed,' she says. 'Don't give me that look, Merce,' she says. 'You said you are leaving.'

'Are you?' Ife says. 'For real?' She looks distraught for a moment, and then the look is gone and a new resolve sharpens her gaze. 'Actually' – she claps her hands – 'actually, can we focus, please. Because this is distracting me. Mercy – what's happening? Should we be looking for these cats?'

30

It would have been nice to have made this beginning last for longer. To have stayed, with no pressure, in this return. But it is different here; the moment has gone, now that Ife has mentioned the cats.

And it sounds worse, as Mercy explains the situation. The girls hardly move as they listen. Only Bessie is still smiling when Mercy finishes speaking. One of her eyebrows is arched in disbelief.

'So yeah,' Mercy says, in conclusion. 'They've just vanished. And the weird thing is I've sat for cats literally so many times and I mean, they're chill. Usually. I have never had cats just straight up disappear.'

They are still standing in the hallway, behind the door. Bessie leans back against the wall and shuts her eyes. Next to her, Ife only looks more confused.

'You're being serious?' Bessie says at last.

'Oh, this is real,' Ife says. 'Mercy. What even.' Then: 'Wait,' she says. 'So.' She closes her eyes, and presses her fingers to her temples. 'You mean you are genuinely here to look after someone's cats?'

'She's a housesitter, right?' Bessie says. 'I read an article about this. People use it to travel. Like Airbnb but free.'

Mercy says yes, this has been her life for the past year.

'Okay, I get it, then,' Ife says. 'Okay. It's connecting. Allow it. I got up early.'

'This is new to me as well,' Joy says. 'So, what. You live in other people's houses?'

It sounds strange like that, but that is the truth of it, Mercy thinks.

'Yeah,' she says. 'I mean, usually I'm in London. This' – she gestures towards the light at the end of the hallway – 'this place is actually the furthest I've been so far.'

'Do you not get lonely?' Joy asks.

She tells them about the network, and Ekua. 'Plan is, from here, I can finally travel.'

'Okay,' Ife says, as she looks back down the hallway. 'Okay. Okay. This is good. So, then. What's the deal? Did you sign a contract or anything? And the homeowner. Is she paying you for this?'

'That's what I was wondering,' Joy says. 'Because, I have to say – you look good. Sis. Your skin. Hair – everything.'

'Yeah. Your hair has grown. A lot,' Bessie says. 'It looks so healthy.'

'Aw, thanks,' Mercy says.

'Focus,' Ife says, clapping her hands again. 'Please. Girlies. Let's focus. Let's get this straight. I want to know how serious this is. Merce,' she says. 'So. Do they pay you?'

'Not exactly,' she says. 'I don't charge.'

'Oh. You do it for free?'

'Although, the client offered.'

'Ei,' Bessie says. 'The client offered to pay you. And then what? You said no?'

'Sis.' Joy looks equally dismayed. They all have the look now. They are all watching, listening, as though they are waiting for the final twist.

'Let me explain,' Mercy says. 'I think she offered because she thought she was asking for a lot. Because this place is so far from everything.'

'True.'

'It's her first time, and she hasn't travelled in a while.'

'Oh,' Bessie says. 'Imagine she gets back and her cats are gone.'

'She will never leave this house again.'

'Imagine.'

Mercy folds her arms. Worry is twisting her stomach.

'Ei. Unimagine it,' Ife says. 'Please. Jokes aside. We have all day. Let's not worry. Plenty of time. We will find them.' She smooths her hands over her jeans. 'And if we don't, I mean, in the worst case, we will just have to buy new cats.'

Bessie snorts. 'You can't say that. Ife, please.'

'How much was she offering, though?' Joy asks. 'Asking for a friend.'

'Joy,' Ife says.

'I don't know; I didn't even ask,' Mercy says. 'I don't ask for pay. Just on principle. And I figured if this client wants to pay, she can help in other ways. She has connections who may need sitters, too.'

'Ahh. Okay.'

'And I like her. She's interesting.'

'Oh?'

'Yeah,' Mercy says. 'But this is why I'm stressed. I have a reputation I'm trying not to destroy.'

She tells the girls about the app. On her phone, she opens the page with her profile, her rating; the app where, these past months, she has gathered reviews. She tells them she has been getting back into photography through this.

'I took, like, no photos when I was in the church,' she says.

'Oh,' Ife says, her eyebrows arching. 'Can we talk about that? Because I saw it on socials, before you disappeared; I saw that you joined.'

'Yeah,' Joy says. 'We need to unpack that. That was the last I saw of you, actually.'

'I wanted to say something,' Ife says. 'But. Well. We'll talk. Hey. Look at us. We haven't even moved from the front door.'

'I want to see your photos,' Bessie says. 'Are you posting them online again yet?'

'Wait, actually, why couldn't you take photos when you were in that church?' Ife says. 'What was going on there? Did they make you sign NDAs?'

'No, nothing like that,' Mercy says. 'Not like that. It was more that they said it's a distraction, vanity, taking photos.'

'Photos?' Bessie says.

'Yeah, I know, but at the time. They were all, like, the world is fallen, passing away. And I had no time; I was working. And after I left. That's how I got into this. To find somewhere to live. And to save again.'

'You should have called,' Bessie says. 'We could have found something together.'

'Hundred per cent,' Joy says. 'Me. I had no idea you were going through it. Mercy. Honestly. I would have invited you to stay with me if I'd known.'

'We hadn't spoken in ages. I was so embarrassed.'

'Babe.'

'Besides,' she says, 'I needed this; I needed to do this,

but for myself. That's why this housesitters' group, and the mentoring, has been so good. I needed to do it like this, for myself. It's like, in some way – this will be corny, but allow me.'

'Uh oh. Here we go,' Bessie says.

'No, honestly. I feel like the world helped me get back to myself. Because it's, like, random people, who for some reason trust me with their homes, and their pets. It has legit restored my faith in humanity.'

'How icky,' Bessie says. 'I'm kidding, Merce. Proud of you. Looks like you have a decent set-up with this place.' She looks down the hallway, towards the coloured glass.

'You do look well,' Ife says.

'Glowing,' Joy says.

'But like you said, living in these houses depends on your reputation?'

'Yeah, exactly,' Mercy says.

Ife steps ahead, starting down the hallway. 'So,' she says, 'we need to start looking. Reviews aside, I'm actually a bit worried this woman could – she could sue you.'

'Ife. Stoppit.'

'She could. If they are missing, because looking after them – those are the terms of you being here.'

'Even if she's not paying?' Bessie asks.

'She could,' she says. Her brows knit together. 'I mean, I'll look it up. I'm sure it's happened before. Negligence. Or breach of contract.' Now she is tapping on her phone, the light of the screen washing her face with a blue tinge.

'Ife,' Bessie says. 'I need a drink first.'

'Same,' Joy says. 'We haven't even seen the place.'

Ife stops typing on her phone and slips it into her pocket. 'Okay. But if these cats have been missing for a week, you don't know how far they might have gone. Or how they might be holding up. They are domesticated, after all. I did some reading the other night and your, uh, client?'

Mercy nods hesitantly. 'Yeah, the client.'

'Your client – she took someone to court not long ago. A few someones. More than a few. And more than a few times, actually.'

'To court?' Mercy says.

'Yes. This, your client,' Ife says.

'She, what, sued someone?'

'Okay,' Ife says. 'I thought this might be news. But. You know about the situation with her ex-husband, right?'

'Why, what's happening?' Mercy says.

'Ladies,' Joy says. 'Ladies. Please. Drinks first?'

'Wait,' Mercy says. 'Hold up. What. The client did what?'

'I looked her up,' Ife says. 'Sure. I know you said not to, when you sent the map. But I was curious; I mean, sis, this place.'

Mercy sinks back against the wall.

'Yes,' Ife is saying. 'I know you said don't look. You want to surprise us. I get it, fine. But.'

'Oh yeah,' Bessie says. 'Mercy, why did you say don't look her up? Did she say that? Or was it just to surprise us?'

'No. No,' Mercy says. 'It's a rule: I don't look clients up.'

She tells them it was awkward, at the start, that it became distracting. That it was easy to get caught up thinking about their lives, and what might have happened in these spaces before. It helps, she says, to keep a respectful distance.

'Where did you look her up?' Mercy asks. 'Was it just online?'

'Yeah,' Ife says. 'I had to dig, but yeah, it was all there.'

'Ife is a stalker. It's a serious problem,' Bessie says.

Ife lifts both hands. 'See it from my perspective,' she says. 'I don't see you for, what, years? Then I get a map – you're in a house in a forest? I had to look. The last I heard, you were joining a cult.'

'No. I get it,' Mercy says. 'I just don't want to get tangled in someone else's life.'

'Guys,' Joy says. 'Let's not stress out. We're good. We have all day.'

'Yeah, but we might not,' Ife says. 'We should look first. I'll feel better, once I know they're in here. Merce, I know you, and don't fight me, but it does look like you're trying to self-sabotage with this. Because you have a nice set-up. But if you lose the cats.'

'Ignore her,' Bessie says. 'She's being dramatic – she's between jobs.'

'Pronounced: gardening leave,' Ife says. 'But what I'm saying is: Merce, I get it. It must be weird to read about someone if you are in their house. I get that.'

'Thank you,' Mercy says. 'It's fine when I'm out. In a few weeks.'

'Out, you know,' Bessie says. 'Is this prison?'

Ife says, 'You have to stay in here, right?'

'I can take walks,' Mercy says. 'We all should, later, actually. There is a lake. We could take pictures there.'

In the kitchen, Bessie arranges the tulips in a vase, and Joy sets out the bottles that she has brought on the worktop. A tall bottle of vodka, and cans of Supermalt.

'Jesu,' Ife says, watching.

'What,' Joy says. 'I heard there's food, so we need drinks.'

'You carried all this from the station?' Mercy says.

'Heroic,' Bessie says.

'You can't pretend the time we made our own cocktails didn't slap,' Joy says.

'Here she goes.'

'We were something,' Mercy says.

'We need music,' Ife says.

She had imagined days like these would be common, that they would always live close – to each other, and to where they grew up. But Joy is the only one who still lives in Enfield.

Though they arrived together, they came from opposite sides of London. Ife lives in Twickenham. Bessie came from her new flat in South London.

'Listen,' Bessie says, and lifts her hands. 'Before you start.'

'I haven't said a word,' Mercy says.

'You,' Ife says, 'the same person who used to hate on South London.'

'Yeah. I was petty. I know.' Bessie leans against the counter, and looks through the glass doors to the garden. Heaviness shadows her gaze. When she speaks again, her voice is soft. 'I only started the whole thing about hating the south when my dad moved there.'

'Yeah?' Mercy says.

'For real,' Bessie says. 'It messed with me, that he. Well. Maybe you know, maybe you heard, but. Well, it turned out he had another family.'

'Wait. A whole other family?' Ife says.

'Yeah.'

'I mean,' Mercy says. 'I heard that he cheated. But what?'

'Exactly,' Bessie says. 'But I'm glad in a way, because, yeah, it was a shock, but in the end that was what made me get help. As in therapy. Guys, I completely crashed at uni. Got to the point where I was looking at my hands and I was thinking, how do I know these are even my hands?'

'Bessie, what?'

'I didn't say. I didn't know what or how to at the time. But then I saw the counsellor. Got a referral for therapy. And honestly, I wish I'd done it earlier; once I saw from a new perspective, it was clear how it had stopped me from trusting other people. This was why I went quiet around that time. I had the sense any guy I liked would just cheat on me. And that they would gaslight me like my dad did to my mum.'

'Sis,' Joy says. 'Hey.' She opens her arms and draws Bessie close.

'We never even talked about this,' Ife says. 'What?'

'I mean, I wasn't ready to talk. End of uni? You girls were smashing it,' Bessie says. She steps back from Joy's embrace, smooths her hands down her jumper.

'Smashing it?' Mercy says. 'Hello. Literally gave up after first year.'

Bessie grimaces. For a moment she looks like the girl she was at secondary school, with her expressive eyes, and her eyebrows knitting with concern. 'Yeah, but,' she says, 'you had a plan. You had your first camera then, right?'

'Yeah, but,' Mercy begins, then changes her mind. 'Actually, sorry. Go on. I interrupted.'

'At the time, I didn't want to bring the energy down. I kept saying, yeah, let's catch up soon. But then, well, there were exams. And then internships. Jobs. And there was always a reason why we couldn't just meet.'

'We've honestly been so rubbish at staying in touch,' Joy says.

'For real,' Ife says.

'I mean, we had a pandemic,' Mercy says.

'Yeah, but before that, we completely lost ourselves.'

They stand in silence. The room is still. From outside, there is the coo of distant birds.

'I'm so glad we're here, though,' Bessie says.

'We should head out,' Ife says. 'For photos.'

She is looking back through the doors out to the garden. Rain is still speckling the glass. Beyond, the sky is luminous grey, the sun hidden yet everywhere.

'Yeah, we can,' Mercy says. 'We can walk out to see the lake as well.'

'Honestly, Merce – this house,' Bessie says.

'Okay,' Ife says. 'So that's a plan. We find the cats, and then photos. Oh. Mercy, is there a map?'

Mercy says that, yes, there is a floorplan on the wall in the study. 'You're right: we need to look,' she says. 'Properly. I kept meaning to look for them, but then I just got lost in doing other things. Even just in thinking. Honestly. I felt like I had slipped out of time or something here. This place is so quiet. I felt like I was losing my mind.'

'I feel like there are lots of small rooms here,' Joy says. 'I can see how a cat could disappear.'

'Three, though,' Bessie says, 'right?'

'Yeah,' Mercy says. 'Two dark shorthairs; one is fluffy – like, cream-coloured? Oyo, Ubuntu and Sankofa.'

'Ei. Intentional,' Joy says.

'First,' Bessie says. 'Before we start. Where is this rice I was promised?'

'Food is for after we find the cats,' Joy says.

'Now why would you say that?' Bessie says. 'Allow it. This is basically lunchtime, no?'

'I'm sure we can find them in an hour,' Joy says. 'Then we can eat at around two?'

'You have pictures?' Ife asks. 'Of the cats?'

'Yeah, we should put up posters in the park.'

'Would they be outside?' Bessie asks. 'Oh. Are there animals here?'

'Animals. You hear yourself? In this UK. What, a badger? A stoat?' Joy laughs.

'Does the homeowner leave instructions?' Ife asks. 'As in, have the cats run off before?'

'Yeah, is it like *Wife Swap* where they leave rules?'

'Loved that show,' Bessie says.

'Same,' Mercy says. 'And yeah. We can look at the guidance later.'

Ife claps her hands. 'Let's go.'

31

On Ife's suggestion, they search in pairs.

'We go from opposite sides,' she says. 'We herd them to the centre – to the hallway?'

'There's a cellar.' Bessie says, still looking at the floorplan.

'For her collection,' Mercy says.

'Ooh,' Ife says.

'We can't go down there,' Mercy says. 'It's locked.'

'This place is complex. I feel like the cats can hide even if we look in pairs. If we could stay longer, though – or is it a rule?'

'Yeah,' Mercy says. 'Sadly no sleepovers allowed.'

Bessie says, 'But cats are nocturnal, no?'

'Yeah,' Joy says. 'Would you not hear them more at night?'

Mercy shakes her head. 'This is the thing. It's dead quiet.'

'Shall we just start?' Ife says.

The plan is fine; it is the execution that falls apart. Each room offers a host of distractions. Mercy looks with Bessie, with Joy and Ife on the phone. It was Joy's idea, to treat this like a serious operation, to use their phones to stay connected as they search. It is like the walkie-talkies they used to play with years ago.

Of course, it is hard to stay serious for long like this. The girls keep asking about the sculptures, and the lights in the dining room. Now, after half an hour of searching, they are out of sync; they are no longer moving in symmetry towards the main hallway. And then there is the signal – or lack of it, the connection faltering.

When they meet in the kitchen, for a break, the plan dissolves. Joy suggests they open the drinks. Supermalt-vodka, for old times' sake.

'Yeah, I need sugar,' Joy says. 'Wilting.'

Mercy suggests they try the fruit crumble.

'It's best warm,' she says. 'Let me heat it up first.'

They sit in the front room around the coffee table. Ife says it is fine to chill for a while. Earlier, in a room at the back, she heard a meow.

'Okay, so maybe it was not a whole meow. But from what I heard, it was definitely a cat.'

'Did you see any of them, though?' Mercy asks. She spoons some of the crumble into a bowl and passes it across to Bessie.

'Thank you, babe,' Bessie says.

'Not exactly,' Ife says. 'But.'

'Ugh. I missed this,' Bessie says, digging her spoon into her helping. 'I need this aroma as a perfume. So good.'

'I heard something, too,' Joy says. 'When we started. But it could have been the wind.'

Behind her, drizzle is beading on the window. The meadow is bright; sun is still breaking through the grey.

'Didn't see them, no,' Ife says. 'It was a cat, though.' She takes the second bowl of crumble from the table. 'But.' She lifts her hand, and licks berry juice off her thumb. 'If you were a cat, and this was your base, and it was raining, would you leave?'

'True,' Mercy says.

'I don't know,' Joy says. 'If my owner disappeared and some random woman replaced her, I might consider it. Ife, you just got distracted, earlier.'

'What? Earlier when?'

'In the room with the painting.'

'Maybe,' Ife says. 'That was an insane painting, though.' She takes a napkin from the table.

'Which painting?' Mercy asks.

'The one in the room with cactuses,' Joy says, accepting the bowl Mercy passes to her.

'Women, fantasy vibes, connected by rays of light. And then light is sort of emanating from the earth?'

'The woman, this collector. She must be set,' Bessie says.

'Yeah. I'm still trying to make sense of this place,' Ife says.

Mercy nods. 'She's been collecting for decades.'

Ife says, 'From what I read, I assumed this woman is just. I would say, petty?'

'Why?' Joy says.

Ife shakes her head. 'Mercy doesn't want to hear it, right? We can circle back later.' She laughs. 'It's a good idea, actually, to enjoy the space without thinking about someone else's drama.'

'You know, it's common for cats to live in many houses at once,' Bessie says. She lifts her glass and sips.

'True.'

'Where is the nearest neighbour, Merce?' Joy says.

'Miles away,' she says. 'There's a pub. I think someone

lives above it. But I don't think the client spoke to many people when she lived here. She was saying it was bad for her, staying here for so long.'

'I can imagine,' Ife says.

'Yeah, cats tend to do whatever,' Joy says. 'I bet they are having their own holiday right now. They can literally disappear and show up eight months later.'

'I still think they are in the house,' Ife says.

32

She had forgotten this: how the girls transform, before the lens. A settling, full repossession of themselves. The camera is balanced on its stand in the kitchen, out of the rain, while they pose, here, in the green.

'If it's a Garden of Eden theme, we need forbidden fruit,' Joy says.

So, back, with leftover berries. Natural with the clicker, to catch these moments between poses, in laughter. At other points Mercy takes the camera in her hands. To frame the girls – together, one at a time.

They change outfits, swapping bracelets, tying Bessie's scarves over their hair.

'Merce. Release the photos quickly, o,' Ife says. 'I need to share them with my mum. Hei. Adulthood.'

'Ei. Adulthood where?' Joy kisses her teeth. 'I still feel like a kid.'

'Is that a bad thing?' Mercy says.

'It's only since I bought the flat that I've felt fully arrived,' Bessie says. 'But I get it, for sure.'

'Hundred per cent,' Ife says. 'I think it's the intentionality; that's what makes your life your own.'

'Yeah, it's also the fact that your girl is still single,' Joy says. 'Pray for me, o. But nah, I'm telling myself not to put pressure on it. Still. It's getting to that point where people are settling down. And I don't know, people see it as a strength. Like, I'm independent or whatever. But honestly, I just have no luck on dating apps.'

'Those apps are hell,' Ife says. 'Delete them, please.'

'The rest of my life is work. Where else am I going to meet someone?' Joy says.

'Sis. It will come,' Bessie says. 'Trust. It will. For me. I'd stopped looking. And Joe. From day one we've just been trading silliness. Goofy as hell. Trust. It will come.'

Joy is still making a face.

'If you want it,' Bessie says, 'it will come. And there's more to life. I think it falls into place when you're content.'

'Preach,' Ife says.

'How about you, Merce,' Joy says. 'And if I can ask, what happened with Gemz?'

Another glass of Supermalt-vodka, and the words come easier. But now, once it is out – how they ended – a weight shifts from her lungs. There is a lightness, shaky as it feels, with the truth.

'Babes,' Ife says. 'We don't have to go there if it's still raw.'

'Yeah, let's not. Good vibes only,' Bessie says.

'No,' she says. 'I want – I think I need to.'

There was no way to talk about it before. There was just the break-up and then the spiral into the church.

In the dining room, the colours of the Moroccan lampshade soften the walls. Over jollof and grilled chicken and kelewele and salad. Passing bowls, scooping more onto their plates. Here they get into it, the heaviness of these years.

Ife says work has been her hardest struggle.

'I get obsessive,' she says, poking her rice with her fork. 'I still feel, in some way – like I need to prove myself.'

'You?' Bessie says. 'To whom?'

Ife pulls a tight smile and lays her fork on the plate. 'It's been like this since my interview. Cambridge,' she says. 'Which is insane. That was a lifetime ago? I don't know. I just. Everyone expected me to get in. The school. Parents. You all saw it.'

The memory is a dull heat in Mercy's chest. The excitement they had all held, anticipation gathering them, and then the weight of it, that pressure cooling, unrealised. The sense of being on the brink of a different world, a cornucopia, a spread of possibilities close enough to feel their shine, reflections scattering from the unseen, there, and then not.

'And when I didn't. I just. I don't even know.'

This, too, they never discussed. There was no space.

'Since then I've felt like I have to prove them wrong? It's like they're haunting me. I used to dream about it. Three men. Literally three old white men. That interview, I felt like an idiot for trying. It was so awkward. So since then, yeah, it started with that. Since then I've just felt I have to prove them wrong. Because I know my stuff. I'm good at what I do. So at times, yeah, I take on too much. And it's part of why I took so long to catch up with you girls. I told myself once I make partner, I'll throw a party. Do something major, and we'll reconnect.'

'I feel that,' Joy says.

'It's tough,' Ife says. 'And there's so much pressure. Sometimes I think – more since I stopped going to church – who is pouring into our cups? But then I think. Well. I think it's hard because I mean, like, we're the first generation born here? Our parents, they love us but they're still figuring it out, too. This is why lately I'm now thinking, hmm. It could be rewarding to have children. I mean, lately I think it would be nice. To pass it on, the lessons from growing up here. Let some of that softness back in, you know? Because my whole family is pressure, all the way.' She snaps her fingers. 'Excellence. Every day. But at some point, you know what, we have to live. And this is corny. Sure. But a big part of what we have – and I'm thinking this is the point – a big part of what we have is here, each other?'

They sit in a warm quiet. Music carries from the speaker in the hallway, the rhythm pulsing softly through the floorboards.

'I wish we had done this earlier,' Joy says.

'So nice here,' Ife says. 'All this space.'

'Oh. I was going to ask. What would you say,' Bessie says, to Mercy. 'What would you say to Gemz if she reached out?'

'Now?'

'Yeah. While you are here. I'm not saying you should use the fact that you are here as a flex or anything, but.'

'She won't,' Mercy says. 'She wouldn't reach out.'

'Okay, but if she did. Hypothetically.'

'When did you two last speak?' Ife says.

Mercy sinks back. Closes her eyes. 'The last time. So. I mean. I sent her a few messages. Ages ago. Just like, how have you been. Do you want to talk about what happened.'

'And?'

'Nothing.'

'What?'

'Yeah. Nothing at all. She's done. She's checked out.'

'Damn,' Ife says. 'That's so odd because I did not get that impression of her at all.'

'Same,' Bessie says. 'That's why I was wondering.'

'She won't reach out. How it happened. I find myself wondering if I ever even knew her; it was so out of character. But yeah, no. If she had wanted to, she would have done it by now. That's part of why I went back into the church. Though I mean, sure, I didn't realise how extra this specific church would be. At the time I was tired of pushing myself over and over, like, to be honest. To go on dates, to show up, because I know what certain people will think. It doesn't matter. I know that, sure, the world will catch up in its own time, and even if they don't, this is my life; I get to live it. I know, but in reality it's so draining when I try, when I gather myself and try and then it ends like this. So I thought. If I join the church, I can get back to my old sense of passion, or purpose, at least.'

'I get that,' Ife says. 'I can see that. Hundred per cent.'

'Nah. I still don't get it. You changed your number as well. When I saw that, I'll be honest,' Bessie says, tapping her fork against her plate, 'when I saw that I did feel some type of way, Mercy. That actually hurt, if I am being real. Because. Like, was that necessary. To cut everyone off?'

'At the time we all did it,' she says. 'Everyone who joined the church. They said it was a sign of our commitment to changing.'

'You vanished off socials, too.'

'Yeah. I wanted to try. Because people seemed happy, everyone was so purposeful there. We had something. Maybe it was just about the sense of community. And it felt like returning to something honest. I had an outlet, before, when I believed. There was joy and love, too. Ife, like you said, about people pouring into our cups? I just wanted to belong, to feel like I was part of something again; I can see that now. And I have this fear. Really old. From when I was with Lily, my first, at uni? And now with Gemz. It's like I push myself and it turns into smoke. For now I want to feel secure, complete in myself. My love is valid. When the time is right, I'll go again. But.'

'You still think about her,' Ife says.

'No.'

'No?'

'No.' Mercy raises her glass and takes a sip.

'No feelings at all?' Ife says.

Mercy winces as she sets her glass back on the table. 'Okay, maybe,' she says. 'Now and then. But this is also because of the way that it happened.'

'How? What do you mean?' Bessie says.

'So other than the fact that, well, she left, since it came out of nowhere, I actually have no reason to believe she was wrong for me.'

'Wait. I need to ask something,' Bessie says, waving. 'Do you believe in soulmates?'

Mercy lifts her glass again and takes a mouthful as she thinks. 'I don't know, actually. I think also, seeing the way my parents committed to each other, how they stayed close, that really made me feel like I could have that, like, for myself.' She has not thought of it like this before, but saying it now feels truthful. 'And at times I thought we had it. We could have. We made sense.'

'You should invite her here,' Ife says.

'What.'

'Ife, don't,' Bessie says.

'You should,' Ife says. 'Why not?'

'No,' Bessie says. 'We don't do that. We don't go back.'

'Invite her,' Ife says. 'Why not? See what she says. You're going to leave the country. May as well.'

'You are fully deranged,' Mercy says.

'I'm saying this,' Ife says, laying her cutlery down, 'because honestly, Mercy, at times it's as if you just want to sabotage your blessings. For real. I think you do. And this is why we need each other. This is accountability. I would want you to call me out if I moved like this as well. Otherwise, what are we even doing here? Invite her. Don't overthink it. Why not? Better to try and find out than to regret.'

'Ife,' is all Mercy can say.

'People live their whole lives saying what if, what if. And you know. You two had something. I'm not saying chase it; if it's over, then it's over, fair. But at least allow yourselves to understand why.'

Mercy looks to Bessie, and then to Joy, but they only smile in agreement.

'She has a point,' Bessie says. 'If you don't actually know why it ended, close it down properly. And you have space here.'

'It's not easy,' Joy says. 'Even thinking about this stuff is hard. But. We can even stay over. Solidarity. Think about it. You deserve answers. Tomorrow. We can stay.'

'You girls. Anyway. No. I'm sorry but you can't stay over,' Mercy says. 'I don't want to break any rules.'

'Does she really care?' Bessie says. 'This client person.'

'What?' Mercy says.

'I'm sure she has other issues on her mind. And if she cares, she needs to chill.'

'Maybe,' Mercy says. 'But it's still her house.'

'She must be set,' Joy says. Her gaze drifts up to the coloured panes of the lampshade. 'One piece of art here could probably settle all your debts.'

Ife looks as though she's going to say more. Instead she frowns and lifts her glass to her lips.

After dinner, they open the wine, to review it, and then they eat the rest of the berry crumble. And not long after, it is time to trade farewells. Mercy calls the cab driver to pick them up.

In the hallway, Ife says she will schedule more meetings soon. She might even have to send out agendas, like she used to do while they were in school.

'I needed this,' Joy says, as she laces her boots up.

And from outside, there comes a toot. The taxi. Here, already.

'We need to get our sleepovers back,' Joy says.

'Honestly,' Ife says.

'Spa nights,' Bessie says. 'We can do nights in for self-care.'

'Need this!'

'Mercy. Honestly. I love you so much. Ugh. I'm so proud of all of us.'

33

When thinking back to this time, this stay in Meadowlight, it will be moments like this that resurface. Here in the lull before, when the day is open, undisturbed. She will think of these as waking moments, new, in this room, on the edge of the present. In the morning, before the rain, when the day is tentative, when memories layer over these fading dreams.

The day after the girls' visit, here in bed in the morning, still warm inside from their company, and from their words, today it is noise from outside that interrupts the calm. Which is strange, for so much noise is hard to comprehend inside this house, so much so that for a while, still lying here, eyes closed in resistance, it is more believable that the sound is not from outside, but that the disturbance belongs to a dream. Here is a form of freedom, the choice of whether to fall back into a dream, or instead to sit up and pull away from the night's hold. But the sound – the interruption – comes from everywhere beyond this room. It is not only noise but movement, grating up from the stillness. The noise builds until it shivers through the boards and trembles through the bedframe. Now that it is here, it is impossible to ignore. The noise, Mercy thinks, of an engine. An old one, too, a vehicle waiting outside at the front.

She sits up. The car will be out on the would-be drive before the meadow, that waiting patch of gravel darkened by rain. It takes a moment to remember who the vehicle might belong to. In this moment it is as though the house is slackening around her. The mattress is too soft, sinking away, as though this bed will melt to nothing around her. She sees herself: here she is, a woman hungover, a body softly aching, tired and alone. A woman in a house whose rooms are laden with value. House of treasures, old and new, of unthinkable worth. And then, as suddenly as it fell, the moment lifts. This does not have to be as complex as it is becoming. The noise outside will have a simple explanation. Yes. The noise will be the van from the website. Waste collectors. The company Bessie called last night, the number she dialled over dessert, as they read the client's guidance pack. She said she would call them to help clear up.

So here is the reason for climbing out of bed, for stretching and pulling a jumper on over her pyjamas. And then she walks out, down the hallway into the living room. Through the window the vehicle's lights are flashing red in the fog of the meadow. She sinks onto the sofa by the voile curtain, to watch it pull up, through the thunder in her head.

Even now, looking out through the glass, not to the drive but to the meadow, here she is looking out as though it might be possible, as though it could be possible not to tip back into the dream, not to sink into the images from last night, but as if it might be possible for something of the dream to surface here. The dream, last night, where Gemz appeared. Not a surprise. If anything, it was inevitable from her last thoughts before sleeping, turning her mind back through the conversation with the girls. Their suggestions: that it might help, to at least try to invite Gemz. To speak to her. Reach out one last time. For closure. More so last night, in the quiet after they left, lying there in the dark, thinking back through memories that have resurfaced over these past days, and, with that, thinking back to the list that she wrote on day one. The hope that this house might be a place for reconnection, closing circles. So on slipping out, finally giving in to sleep, it was inevitable that her thoughts echoed with more memories. In the dream, Gemz was outside, in the meadow.

On her phone, new messages wait in the girls' chat.

Bessie wants to know if the cats have reappeared. She says last night was special. They need to do this again. She wants advice on her wedding plans. Says she keeps pushing it back, it is overwhelming.

Ife has sent the photos she took with her phone. Says that her head is punishing her. She just woke up. Thankfully she has all day to follow up on all they had no time to talk about yesterday. Such as, yes, the wedding, and how – or whether – to speak to an ex.

She has followed with a block of solid text, no emojis.

Mercy sets the phone down on the coffee table. There will be time to think about that later.

For all its noise and light, the waste truck itself is small. It backs up further and then the rumbling stops. The front doors open, and two men climb out. Something about their movement connects them. Father and son. Something rhymes across their features.

On opening the door, both men are shorter than they seemed.

'Hello,' they say. The older man adds, 'She got away? The professor.'

Mercy says yes, the woman who is usually here is away. She will be back soon.

'Ha. Told you,' he says to the younger, with a smile.

They are still just standing there, below the step.

'Are you,' the older man says, his glassy eyes on her. 'You're the daughter?'

'Daughter? No,' she says.

The client has not mentioned a child. She has said nothing about family besides her ex-husband. Daughter. The idea sits strangely in her mind. More so with the look these men are giving her, caution mixed with curiosity.

They follow her down the hallway to the kitchen.

'Looks like someone had fun,' the younger man says.

She can see it through their eyes now: the wine bottles. Empty glasses. The unwashed plates in the sink. The bottle of vodka by the window.

She points out the bags that are ready for collection.

They carry them out easily in one trip.

'Same again anytime you need it, love,' the younger man says.

'Have a good one,' the older man says.

She had planned to spend the rest of the day in bed, to pass the hours recovering, and working through light prep for class. Checking the list, to see what to try next in this stay. More cooking, perhaps, before braving the call to Mother. It feels easier already, within the glow from yesterday with the girls. The simplicity of the past, the closeness: reachable. She had meant to go slowly today, to keep things moving in the right direction. And the photos: best to upload them today, too. Bessie always complains if anyone hoards photos of her for too long.

She had meant to sleep. But after the van, the house feels too awake. So she leaves the room and walks the hallway once again. Yesterday's busyness might have enticed the cats out of hiding.

She walks from the stained-glass panels by the garden to the front door. Still, there is no sign. She looks through the peephole in the front door, out to where Gemz stood in last night's dream. She presses her fingertips against the cold wood of the door.

Back to the room – to the en suite for a shower. Today is a good time to try the new conditioner. She opens the bottle and inhales its sweetness. A memory: Ekua suggesting a channel to vlog about natural hair.

She said: 'I feel like we need that energy back. When everyone was uploading montages of their hair growth?'

Early YouTube, she added, was the pinnacle of honesty, when people shared candid footage from their homes. 'It was so healing, right?'

Mercy said hundred per cent. She felt it, too. It took years before her mother let her cut her relaxed hair. And videos from those early YouTubers, women, in the States, caring for their hair, trying new styles, discovering their textures for the first time: those videos helped her – and the girls – make the case.

Perhaps she will start it, the channel, soon; perhaps she

will reach out to the woman who made this conditioner to see about working together.

Now she is thinking of Efia and Mother back at home, about the pictures they used to send of natural hair styles. In the months after her big chop, they sent her suggestions they had collected for new looks. The back-and-forth, only partially joking, and her own attempts to convince them to do the same. In response Mother just laughed and said she had no time for her own hair, with work and church, she had no time to try it out and, anyway, she preferred her wigs. They suited her better, she said. And Efia, who still, after countless burns from chemicals, relaxed her hair, although she said, 'If you stick with it, yeah, maybe I'll try.'

'It's not just about the hair itself,' she remembers saying on those calls with Ekua. And she got it; she was excited about it, too.

Those conversations. How reassuring – how true – they were.

Beneath the falling water, excitement buzzes across her skin.

Out of the bathroom, she lies on the bed, on her stomach. On her phone are more messages. From Bessie:

Yo. Photos please Madame?

And:

wish we could have had more time.

And earlier, from Joy:

Oh. We left bare wine open!

And here, from Ife:

So? Can I reach out? I'm just here doing nothing. I still have her number.

At this, she mutes the group chat.

Instead, she opens a browser. To ask the internet. Because other people will have been in situations like this before. Others will have shared reflections on what to do. Whether it is ever sensible to reach out to an ex.

She is scrolling through a page on Reddit when it appears: a new email from the client.

34

In a way, she has been waiting for this to happen since their first call. It was clear that the client missed her cats. That she was struggling, disorientated, away from the house.

Still, it is startling to read in so many words. In the study now, because she has set a boundary, has decided not to handle correspondence like this in the bedroom. A line she drew in part for the fear of what it might translate to in dreams, for, whether or not it is true, the client's warnings about dreams. This is the first room since university that has felt so clear, and untainted.

She rests her palms on the desk.

Even the email's wording, the stream-of-consciousness flow, is the same as it was in the last email.

She needs to see her cats. Soon. For perspective. These past few days, the client writes, have been exhausting. They have left her on the brink. She is tired from countless attempts to rewrite her speech. She is starting to believe that travelling to New York was a mistake. That she should not have travelled so far after staying for so long in Meadowlight. She writes that now she is here, in New York, looking back on the past years of her life, now that she has spent some time reflecting on her career, which, she writes, increasingly she has found to be inextricable from her life, here, looking back on the past decades, on her interests, her ambitions, all that she has started and failed to complete, she feels as though she is teetering on the edge of a collapse. The trouble, the email continues, is that too much has changed too quickly. She had hoped for this to an extent, that saying yes to this opportunity to speak might help to shock her out from the rut, to break from the isolation that had held her since the pandemic. She had hoped that the shock – the change – would be worthwhile; though she had hoped for this, she fears, now inside it, now that it is happening, she feels as though she has pushed herself too far. Change is good, she writes. But lately she has wondered if New York was too much too soon. Perhaps she should have visited friends in the UK first. In a town, or a quieter city. Yes, New York is too much. It is as though the city, her email reads, for all its beauty, its immensity, it is as though New York itself has changed beyond recognition; the city has shed its skin, perhaps a thousand times, the city has shed its skin and grown a stranger one. And she realises she had not imagined it would change, had imagined that she would find the place largely familiar, that a kind of restoration might come with this, that she might find traces of past delight throughout these weeks, and now she realises how foolish the idea was. Silly to imagine the city might hold still, that it might hold something of her memories, as she had, in her mind, and she is aware that at this point this email is a ramble, but it feels important, she writes, it feels important to set this out, and perhaps this process will help her clarify her thoughts before she attempts to finish the speech one last time.

It feels more unsettling for the significance she had ascribed to returning.

This was, she writes, the city where she fell in love. The place in which living took on an urgency. Here, in love. With a man, sure, the man she later married, and whom she has recently divorced. He was an art dealer then, who had travelled from London, too. She fell in love with him in New York, but this city is also special because it is the place where she fell in love with the world.

New York, just like London, held notes of innumerable other places, her email reads. It was a revelation to her young mind when she first travelled here. Reflections of countless places across its armour of mirrors. She went in search of this again, today. Another dérive, she writes, to clear her head. She walked aiming for nowhere, and found herself lost. And on the map on her phone she saw herself as she was, as a small circle in the grid of avenues, a pulsating dot on a screen moving to nowhere.

How different it was from the first time she got lost here, and though she felt terrible then, now, looking back, there is some comfort in the symmetry of it. Her life began here, the life she chose purposefully. In New York she committed to collecting and archiving, in search of honesty. From here she lived in search of the sacred, perhaps of beauty itself, and it was there, on her walk, years later, as she turned her speech over in her mind, it was there that she saw how far off her life has drifted.

She has been thinking, she writes, this is not about the speech. The speech is a means of illuminating something more. The speech is not as important as she had hoped it might be. She suspects the university invited her for appearances, and for her work here in the past.

Most troubling, and this prompted her to email, she writes, though, yes, she had meant to keep the email short, but it was more honest, letting words flow, as she might have done on a call, or in person, or any other natural way, but that aside, most troubling lately have been her dreams. She has dreamed, these past nights, of her cats. She wakes with the feeling that they are as lost as she feels, no doubt a reflection of her own state of mind; still she cannot shake the feeling that they are unhappy too, that she has ruptured something vital in leaving them in Meadowlight. She felt so troubled with it last night that, when morning came, she almost opened her laptop to book a flight back to the UK. The thought of staying another two weeks here troubled her, and she questioned the value of pushing through it. Her real work, her legacy, is there, in the house. Could they have a call? She needs to see her cats.

After reading the email, Mercy stands and leaves the desk.

Back downstairs, in the kitchen, she looks out through the glass doors to the haze of green.

She gathers the open bottles of wine into a corner. Empties one into a mug.

She was going to drink the leftover wine anyway. It would have been a waste to leave this much wine unfinished. Even if it is nothing to the client.

After, on her phone she emails the client back. Sure, they can speak in an hour or so.

Better, like this. To get it out. Because the cats are not here, that is the truth. More wine, then, for luck.

Her head is foggy when her phone rings. Her throat tightens, but to her surprise it is Ife's photo that fills the screen.
She declines, and sends:

Can't chat atm. What's happening?

In response, Ife sends:

Hey. So. I've messaged Gemz. I've just said you're leaving the country soon and interested in catching up. You can thank or kill me later, haha.

And moments later:

Also, I have found more about your client. Her daughter? Are you ready?

35

And Ife was right. In some ways the girls can see each other more clearly than they can see themselves. Because this, too, like Ife said yesterday, this is another example of her tendency to self-sabotage. The refills of wine, before returning now, back up to the study for this call. Late, with that, by half an hour. Here with this sluggishness, and this numbness. It is as though new doors stand open in her mind. First, there is the door busy with Ife's messages, messages that are still trickling in on the phone there on its shelf under the desk, links to articles and even a video, all of which presumably detail whatever scandal Ife has uncovered, the messages keep buzzing despite her reply to say no, she cannot deal with reading this yet, not now, not today, she does not want to hear more details about the client's life or her daughter. Now may be the worst time to see whatever Ife has found, now, while facing the client on the call to explain herself. Why she is late, why the cats are not here. But Ife is Ife, and so more messages come in, until, yes, she takes the phone from the shelf and mutes this chat as well.

But beyond this, another door stands open, a door that

is open to the silence around Gemz. Not long ago she swiped down through her messages – just to look at Gemz's profile picture again. She is still here, on this old number. Ife said Gemz read the message that she sent earlier today. And while looking, here in the study, she saw Gemz typing. Then nothing. Typing again, only to stop.

Distracting.

She is here, in the study, now. On the call, with the client's face on the screen, both their faces in neat squares. She takes a sip of water. Better to get it out now, before the client notices and says it first. She sips again and sets the glass on the desk.

On the screen, the client is still talking. She has been talking since the call began.

Mercy was ready, prepared to explain; she is ready to say it: the cats are not here. They are missing. That she and her friends looked for them yesterday with no success. She is ready to say it now. But the client will not stop talking. She is talking, in circles, about New York. It sounds as though the city has transformed again since her last email. This time it seems to have redeemed itself, improved, for now she is talking about how good it felt not long ago, how good it was to venture outside on another walk; as though she has caught up with herself after the flight at long last, and now an overflow of words is cascading in her mind, a new understanding, as happened before when she first travelled here. Like this, it seems as though she could talk on and on for hours, branching off, away from her own ideas in tangents.

Again, she raises the glass, rests the rim against her lip. Another sip of water, to mute this frustration. This work is simple. This is easy. To stay. Watch the pets. Keep the house. Do everything it takes to reassure the client.

On the screen the client says her new speech is flowing more naturally now. The old structure had proved unworkable, she says. It was too rigid. There was too much she wanted to say.

Her voice softens; her tone is lighter, questioning. As though she is understanding this for herself in real time. This is, she says, a significant milestone for her. It will be her first event since she lost her tenure. She says she realises the shock is just catching up with her now. She had no time to process it before, in the house.

'It was sudden,' she says. A shadow crosses her face. Her hair is up in a purple scarf. Her eyes are lined in black. She wears no glasses and no jewellery on this call; there is no shine, no movement about her now.

'At the time,' she says, her gaze low again, 'at the time, I wasn't ready to accept how much it stung. I mean, it's a space. A university. A network. But it is a platform; it elevates – do you see that? I told you about my father,' she says. 'About his parents. Well. There was an understanding – there was a fair deal of hope for what I might do with my life. Because it interested me when I was small: the movement, the legacy. My mother's side, her brother – sent me to a good school. Now I look back, it was all very alienating. I think that is part of why I held so tightly to the past. It is rare for people to change, I think. It's easier to move around and do the same. To call it something new because it's in a different place. And perhaps it is, because it fits a different environment, but it still fits; it's the same underneath. Well. My father's friends brought me gifts from their travels. Once people know what you enjoy, you attract more of it. And at school I mixed with girls who liked to go to auctions. We would dress up and try perfumes. Well.

When we went they liked to play, to raise their hands, to bid, to push the numbers. But we went for the atmosphere, the *want* in those places. You could feel how much the bidders wanted a piece. I loved it, and yet there was something grubby in it, the stream of numbers. The idea – something in it repulsed me. There I go. What was I saying? Yes. I grew into different circles with that. But I'd always believed it would amount to more.

'I first travelled to Benin when my grandmother passed. That was where I learned of the Bronzes. I never imagined they would return in my lifetime. But by then, I had become estranged from the faculty. They didn't like my ideas. And then with the pandemic, I had too much time; I think that was it. I did get into a few disagreements online.

'And when I lost my position I told myself I had expected this.'

She says it happened there, in the study. An email, and a call. Gone. She has been reflecting on what it meant to belong while redrafting the speech.

'I did not – well, I could not – see. Life just happens, until you step away from it. With the pandemic, I did make that house – well, that house became – my life. The collection. And. Well. I have no one to continue my work.

'Anyway, I meant to say this has been a process. The speech needs more work. But I have space. I need to stop worrying; it's a terrible habit. Much to do! Oh. This has been helpful. Mercy, I'm so glad you're there. Really. I don't think I would have escaped the house otherwise.'

'I'm glad, too,' Mercy says.

'Oh. Before I go, how are my cats behaving? They're not around, are they? Are they still downstairs?'

Mercy folds her arms on the desk. Here it comes. She

clears her throat. 'Yeah,' she says. 'So the last time I saw them they were downstairs.'

'Ah, they're downstairs. Of course they are.'

She had meant to explain more, but the client looks satisfied. And, she tells herself, this is most likely to still be true. 'Yeah,' she says. 'The last I saw, they were in the hallway. I thought about trying a call from downstairs, but the WiFi—'

'Yes, unfortunately you won't have much luck with that downstairs. Aw. Well. It would have been nice. To see them. But I know how hard it can be to get the three of them together. Look, I want to get back to work while I'm still in flow. Let's leave it there for now. But please send over the photos as soon as you can. Let's speak again soon. Enjoy the rest of your day.'

'You too,' she says. 'And good luck with the speech.'

When the call ends, she rests her head on her arms on the desk and closes her eyes. For a moment, all is calm. When she opens them, light is flashing from below. On the shelf underneath the desk, the phone screen is blinking with a call.

36

Ekua. Never has her appearance on the screen brought so much relief. Though at times it feels as though she knows exactly when to call, as though she can tell there is a crisis unfolding.

'Crisis? How? What's happening?' she says, when Mercy takes the call and mentions this.

Mercy sinks back into the chair and rests her eyelids. She can feel the room pulsating around her. The air is close with the pressure of more rain yet to fall, and the tartness of wine clings in her throat. Underneath the silence, she can feel another headache beginning. When she opens her eyes the light from the computer singes them. She sits up and props the phone on the desk by the laptop. Explains to Ekua there is still no sign of the cats. It is likely, she says, that by now they are lost. The client called just now, she tells Ekua; they just spoke.

'I'm literally shaking here,' she says. She lifts her hand, watches the fingers trembling over the desk. 'Because I haven't told her yet.'

On the phone screen, Ekua's eyes widen.

'I tried,' Mercy says. 'But Ekua, this client has so much to say. And then it was like she was ready to move on and get back to work? Like maybe she's not worried at all. She went from saying she was having dreams about the cats, omens, that kind of thing, to saying she's back in flow, everything's good now. Carry on.'

'Wait, wait,' Ekua says. She is seated now, in a dressing gown, on a rattan chair. It is still morning in her world, and her eyes look softer, still unlined. She sweeps her hair back and tucks it behind her ear. 'Mercy, what is happening? What is going on? Talk to me.'

Mercy props the phone against the monitor. She sits back from the desk to explain. 'The girls were here yesterday. They came up from London for the day. And yeah, we looked. Well, sort of. We tried.'

On the screen, Ekua bobs her head. 'That's why I called,' she says. 'I wanted to hear how it went.'

'Yeah, it was really nice,' Mercy says. 'It was special, seeing them again after so long. There was so much to talk about. We just picked up where we'd left off. It was so chill. I just wish we could have had more time.' She leans her arms on the desk again, and sinks a hand into her 'fro. The coils are still damp, and soft with the new conditioner. 'Even just more time to look through the house thoroughly. But it was great. Really special. Oh, that reminds me. I still need to upload the photos. But. We had fun. I wish I'd done it earlier.'

'I'm glad,' Ekua says. 'That sounds so wholesome and chill. But what's happening today? So, what, you and your friends looked together, and you still did not find the cats?'

'Exactly. I mean, we may have heard them. But we haven't seen them, no.'

'I'm confused. Last time we spoke, you said you were going to set up some cameras, right?'

The ache in her head grows louder with this reminder. 'Yeah,' she says. 'It's more that I was thinking with the girls here, we would find them easily.'

'So you didn't set the cameras up?'

'I should have. I got caught up thinking about everything, getting ready.'

'Merce,' Ekua says. She clasps her hands together. 'Please. Tell the client.'

It feels as though the day is stretching endlessly. As though the strain of its reach is inside her, too. She checks the time in the corner of the screen – it's only five. She reaches for the glass of water, only to find it depleted.

'You need to tell her,' Ekua says. 'Just tell her, please.'

'I will,' she says. 'I will. I meant to just now. But I mean. If I had told her earlier, from what she said – like, from how she has been struggling with her speech and with New York – if I'd told her the last time we spoke, I'm pretty sure she would have cancelled her stay and flown back already.'

'Mercy,' Ekua says, her voice gentler. 'You need to tell her. You're making this more complicated than it needs to be. You have a great place. Please don't let it slip because of something you can control.'

'I know. You're right. I will,' Mercy says. 'I have a friend who might be coming up to visit soon. We can look together. When she is here. Well, she is more than a friend, but we were friends before.'

On the phone screen, Ekua's eyebrows climb. 'Your ex?'

'We were chatting about it,' she says. 'Yesterday. I was chatting about it with the girls. It got me thinking.'

'You are going to invite your ex,' Ekua says. 'Wait. Have you been drinking?'

'A little. I mean I will sleep on it. I haven't invited her yet.

I get it. I know how it sounds, but I want to try something.' And it is true, now that she has said it. It could help for closure. At least to try. 'I do want to speak to her, before I leave, to close it down. I feel like I need to do this. Honestly, I've just been thinking about her so much here.'

On the screen, Ekua's eyebrows knit together. She looks ready to interrupt, to say something, but instead, she stays quiet and inclines her head.

'I want to try to speak to her again before I leave,' Mercy says. 'There are so many loose ends I want to sort out. I've been thinking. You know, in a way, the break-up was what got me into housesitting to begin with. I feel like with this sit, I finally have enough space to try.'

Ekua is still watching in silence from the phone screen.

'I think here I'm distant enough from where things fell apart to look at it again. If I get nothing else from this, I want to try.'

37

Since the split she has imagined meeting Gemz multiple times. Often, in these scenarios, when they meet, it happens by coincidence. Often the meeting is fleeting and in transit – in the roar and clanking of the Jubilee line or in the busyness on the platform. In some versions they meet at Baker Street, where Gemz used to stop to change lines on her way home. Or further south – other times they meet at London Bridge. They meet on the way to the market where she and Gemz used to go on Saturdays with good weather, where they would queue for paella or fried rice. They see each other amidst the flavours and heat from the food stalls. Or, in other scenarios, they meet on the bridge itself.

In the first weeks after Gemz left, she considered going to look for her. To ask her in person what she had been thinking, and why she was ignoring so many messages and calls. She considered going back to the cafe where Gemz worked. She thought about walking by just to check that Gemz was still in London, the cafe she used to love complaining about on Saturdays, together slow-waking, cosy in bed, when they used to talk back through the drama of the week; in the cafe, always a madness, Gemz liked to say, though she also said she had started working there for her sanity – to counter the alienation she felt from her other job. Her other job was predictable, at least, she said, answering queries for a skincare start-up. The start-up was based in Bristol; she had never met her colleagues in person, and it was unlikely that she ever would. It added up somehow, she said. It balanced out. It was part of the plan to save up to travel. And it helped that this job was remote, she said. It meant that she could work from anywhere with power and WiFi. Alas, its rootlessness also made that work all-consuming. Gemz: answering emails through dinner, upon waking, and even tapping out messages behind the till at the cafe. People message me from a void, she used to say; they message or call and just complain. Followed by: I mean, I am not complaining about it; I am just saying, this is the exact kind of work that is designed for a robot, you know? And part of me thinks that is exactly what I'm becoming.

To feel like a person again, she said, she took the second job. Afternoon shifts at the cafe inside the station – where they met.

She has imagined meeting Gemz multiple times through these past months, at times purposefully, other times in dreams. She has tried to imagine how it might go, and where it could happen, and when, but for all these scenarios, she has never imagined that they would meet again in a house. A private space sealed off – theirs, for a while. And especially not a house like this. Not a place so open, with enough time and quiet around them to speak and listen. Properly. To see each other. It is too much to imagine: a conversation, a meal with Gemz – here. But she is here, as good as here, her message reads.

Her message has just come in, moments ago, here in the quiet before sunrise. Mercy reads it on her phone, as she sits up in bed. She reads the letters again, and again just to be sure.

If you're up for meeting, shout. I'm there.

She thinks of Gemz, sitting up looking at her phone, too. Gemz, reading these same words again, perhaps, as she waits for a response.

38

A new nervousness surrounds her as she stands before the door. Gemz, outside. Different, too, with this view through the peephole, distorted with the curve of the lens. There. Still Gemz. Her hands fidget with her jacket, and go up to fuss with her hair. Her dreads are longer, loose about her shoulders.

But, somehow, she is here.

Mercy braces herself, and opens the door.

After the hug, fitting together, muscle memory – unplanned, for if anything she had decided to keep her distance – after Gemz has shed her coat and removed her boots in the hallway, now they are here, in the front room; they settle in the armchairs by the coffee table.

She had planned to show Gemz around the house. She had thought of going to the kitchen first – to start with some wine. For although it is still early, just after lunch, a drink will help with these nerves, and it is not as though anyone is here to judge them for it. This day has come – and is happening – too quickly. She had not expected Gemz to show up the day after sending that message, after their brief exchange – about the where and when, though not the why; they were careful in those messages, to leave the details to talk through in person. She had not expected Gemz to get a ticket at such short notice and to come up so soon. But it is best like this. Wait long enough and likely they would have put it off, again and again. Now Gemz is here, in the front room, gazing at the speaker in the corner.

'I can put some music on,' Mercy says. 'I think it works.'

Gemz is already up, heading for the speaker. 'This is why I came up, you know,' she says, glancing back. She leans down towards the speaker's controls and her dreads hang over her face. Just as she used to do when nervous, hiding in busyness. Still, it is hard not to smile watching her.

'For what,' Mercy says. 'You came up for this speaker?'

'Yeah,' Gemz says. 'This particular speaker. For real, though. I want to play you something.' She glances up again, a question in her gaze.

Over wine, Gemz says she has been working on a soundscape. She says it is a commission. Her first.

They are sitting again, on opposite armchairs, legs tucked up. The blossom is pretty, Gemz says, she enjoyed it on the walk here from the station. She has been meaning to take a trip like this lately, to take a break and get away from London for a bit. The blossom is pretty, but the day still has its chill. She sips her wine and says she would like to go for a walk soon, into the park. It might be nice to walk, in rain or sun.

'Oh. Is your mum still collecting those photos of lakes?' Gemz asks. 'And how is she? Have you sent her any photos from here?'

'Yeah. I need to,' Mercy says. 'I need to call her, actually.'

Gemz looks on the cusp of saying more, but instead she raises her glass and sips.

'It's so quiet here,' Gemz says. She says she has been recording silences on her Dictaphone, which she takes out from her pocket, a black remote. She says she has been collecting silences, layering it for her soundscape.

She tips back the remainder of her wine. 'Okay, let me play this. Here. Listen to this. I recorded some of this on the train here and layered it in. You can hear the movement.'

A rush of softness pours through the speakers. The sound of a breeze washing through a chasm. A rhythm pulses underneath, a steady beat.

Mercy closes her eyes.

'I wanted to say,' Gemz continues, 'before your friend messaged me, I was sure you never wanted to see me again.'

When Mercy opens her eyes, Gemz is looking away, out through the bay window. The rain appears to have stopped.

'Shall we go?' Mercy says. 'Shall we just go now? For a walk?'

39

The rain has not so much stopped as thinned. Drizzle, like so much glitter, falls in every direction.

It is here, as they walk, that Gemz eases up.

In the movement, under the sky, she settles into herself. As it went on those walks, a lifetime earlier, in London, when it was impossible to imagine all they could find and lose. Words flow as they once did. Words that circle around all that has changed. And it begins with what remains.

Gemz is still in London, though, yes, she took a pause. She moved to Brighton, right after the break-up. She had to get away, for perspective, but now she is back, staying in Forest Hill; a friend found her a converted studio to rent. A bed in a kitchen, maybe, but it serves for now. She is still DJing, she says. More often than she was before. There is more time, now that she no longer works in customer service. She still has her regular weekend sets in Brixton, she says, though the vibe is different now. Everything is, after the pandemic, she says. And the crowds. People are different there, too. Now that she thinks of it, her style – the rhythm of her sets – has changed. She says it is more about ambience these days.

'For a while I've wanted to change things up.'

They are walking slowly now, as the path slopes uphill. The incline is steep and, beneath their boots, the mud is studded with pebbles. Gemz says she realised that she still had a lot of anger. That anger was tightening around her in the sound. That she kept shifting with it. Leaving jobs, switching venues, moving through different flats.

'I had to get my wisdom teeth out a while ago. Was in bed for, like, two weeks. I thought about us a lot then.' She says she noticed then how jagged her sets had grown. 'I didn't notice when I was inside. People loved it. You get caught up.'

The path narrows here, so they walk in single file. Gemz leads the way, and light flashes gold over the buckles of her backpack. The path glistens from the day's rain; here and there, it vanishes into puddles.

Gemz looks back over her shoulder. She says when she recovered after surgery, she focused more on slowing down.

'If I'm honest,' she says, and shifts her pack up. 'And I want to be. Sometimes I tell myself stories because I want to live in them?'

Here, the path widens again, enough to fall back into step. It is there again: the alignment of their bodies.

Gemz says she started a drumming class with a friend. 'My buddy Lake. Remember him?'

Mercy thinks back but Gemz's friends are a blur. They are so many faces caught up in flashing light. They are people from dating apps, from protests and raves. People who showed up in different permutations for her sets.

She says she and Lake talked about trying the class for months, so they finally just did it; they started it with the new year. And now it is growing. It is still early, she says, but they are working with two schools and a youth club at the moment. Lake is looking into getting sets at a festival for summer.

'We're thinking of outdoor sessions. For all ages. No experience required. Super chill.'

It is different, she says. Making music with a drum. Feeling the rhythm under her hands.

'But you know, it's what I needed then.'

'That sounds good. That sounds beautiful,' Mercy says.

They walk on. The path is clearer; the mud is flattened smooth, the ground pressed wide by countless others. Ahead, the way opens, and the canopy overhead thins; the earth is dappled with light.

'How about you?' Gemz asks. 'What's happening with you? You're back at church?'

No, Mercy says, she is no longer back at church. Though, yeah, she was; she went back for a few months. It was more of an interlude, looking back, a diversion. But that, she says, is a long and messy story.

Gemz laughs. It's fine, she says. We have all day.

So she begins, here again, at the start.

Back to the season that led to these houses. The visit to see Auntie E, with rainbow ice cream in Wood Green, and the walk back and the preacher at the crossing with his leaflets, the leaflets that led them to show up to a new church, a church that was close enough to become Auntie E's new regular. A new church in Turnpike Lane, overspilling with Ghanaians, and both of them, on that first day back, in their kabas and slits, purples and greens patterned over blues, old fits a friend of the family had sewn for a christening, years ago, in matching colours that marked them as family, cloth they had tried on in the living room of Auntie E's flat, half in jest. They tried those outfits on at first to see if they still fitted, if they still made sense after all the years. If these old patterns could still hold them after all that had changed, if their threads could still hold their movement as they once had. And they did fit, and better than before – no accident, it turned out: the fit was intentional; the seamstress had made those fits with room for expansion, space to grow into with the years, space for blessings. And then as they stood, dressed, adorned, in the front room, from there it had seemed wrong to remove these colours, to tone these outfits down before going out to church. It seemed dishonest to go as muted versions of themselves.

Ha. If we were in Ghana, Auntie E said, and laughed.

She had stopped going to church with Mercy's mother years ago. They had argued, disagreed over an issue that neither of them could ignore. From what Mercy heard, from their conversations with other relatives, it was something about the reasons behind Auntie E's divorce. No one had explained it in any more detail than this, for they could not agree on a single retelling. All Mercy knew was that Auntie E had left her husband abruptly, and within months she had stopped joining them for church every Sunday. Only her fall, on the escalator at King's Cross, on her way home from work, only this had prompted Mother to reach out and speak to her again.

And how good it felt that morning on the way to church, even before they stepped outside, taking photos in the lift, with their colours and jewellery doubled in the mirror. A return: to a new church – the first, in Turnpike Lane. It was as surreal as travelling back in time. That old feeling enveloped them, from previous Sundays together, in the richness of Auntie E's perfume, backpack full of leaflets to hand out after service, leaflets they had printed with photos from previous events, any occasion that called for food. There was a sense, in this return, of all the returns that might soon follow. All the connections that could be remade from then on, and with that the understanding that it had to begin with this. That newness would begin with church, there, within the source that vanished in its own light. And that day, for the first time since the break-up, she felt present. It was almost enough to feel certain again. Familiar songs carried the service, and how full the sound became in the smallness of that hall; as the congregation became one with the band, with their tambourines. She can remember the motion of the place. How much they needed it.

She stops walking, for here the light has changed. The sky is closing, blotting away its glare. And now the rain is quickening around them. Standing still, she lifts her palm and sparks of cold sting her skin. The view ahead blurs with the mist, a haze of green and black. She pulls her hood over her hair.

Gemz steps closer. She has no hood to hide under.

'Shall we head back?' Mercy says.

Gemz turns and looks down the path. 'No,' she says. 'I like this.' She tilts her head up, and her dreads fall down her back. 'It's atmospheric.'

They walk on, and then stop again, this time in a clearing of flat mud beneath a dense canopy. They stand together by the blackened wood of a bench. No rain is falling through the foliage overhead, and the air is still and damp.

Mercy tells Gemz about the relief of that first day back, the lightness she felt at that church with Auntie E. It was the same the following week, and then again. Later, they returned during the week for Friday-night prayer meetings, and to help the Saturday building maintenance team. Auntie E was still off work at that time, and she wanted to keep busy as well. Besides that, it helped to feel useful again. They met new people; it was a parallel life that, had they stayed, might have blossomed.

Auntie E made the move first, and left the church, weeks later. She left for a healing crusade at another church. She said it would be a nice day out in a new church, even if nothing came of it. And she took leaflets, as they used to do together; she said she was planning to start catering again.

It was not the same without Auntie E. So it was easy, in the weeks that followed, to move on. More so when a girl invited her to join another church. The girl, a woman – twenty-three – said she was back as a one-off for her mother's birthday. She said that she had grown up in that church, although it had been smaller then, and they had been in a different building. She had been baptised here, in this congregation, with others her age who had also since moved on. She said that this place had once been like home, but over the years all of them had grown up and left. The youth of that church, those who still believed, had gone on to form a separate congregation, a movement that reflected more of who they were; in the music and the teachings it held more relevance for their lives, and now they belonged to that newer congregation. So, with this, Mercy followed to see where the younger believers had gone.

'Ah. Okay. So I'm guessing this is the part where it went wrong,' Gemz says.

Mercy laughs. She stops walking and shifts her bag across her shoulders. She has brought four lenses, two for portraits and the other two for the view over the water. They continue up the path that leads towards the lake.

'Okay, so with this next church,' Mercy says. 'Where do I start?'

She can still remember the excitement of getting ready. It was different then, alone, to go out to meet believers who would all be around her age. 'I had never seen anything on its scale.'

'What, the building?'

'In a way, but no, not really. It was more about the atmosphere.'

'Fair.'

'I mean, the building was nice as well; it was in a theatre, the first service I went to. But the venue kept changing; it was like a pop-up event. This was more of a movement, if that makes sense. The music. The lighting. Every service was like a show. And people were kind. People seemed genuine. I think if I had stayed with it, I could have believed. Fully again.'

'What?' Gemz says.

'It's hard to explain. The atmosphere. I really thought we were doing something.'

'What was it like?' Gemz asks. 'The people, I mean?'

'They were liberal. They seemed open. And creative. The music, the sermons. I could see myself staying there. Growing.'

'And so where did it go wrong – what, it was a scam?' Gemz says.

Mercy winces. 'It was more the financing . . .'

'Financing?'

'They told us to give – as in, to give an offering. It was a tithe, but as time went on, they just kept asking for more.'

'Damn.'

'It got to the point where they had us taking out loans.'

'Loans?'

'Exactly.'

She tells Gemz about the houses. It has been so long since she has even thought of them. But there is no shame, no embarrassment in it here. Though, yes, with hindsight, it was too easy, too straightforward to have been clean.

'They bought houses, renovated them and sold them on. We all invested together. We used to call it kingdom-building.'

'Kingdom-building.'

'And it was. It was all about investing in ourselves. Building something. And it worked, or it seemed like it would. But I mean, they were using us, using our credit. We all lived together, it was fun at the time; they had these houses where we would live together to save, to make sure we could put everything into building the kingdom.'

She tells Gemz about the WhatsApp group with other former members of the church. About how every few weeks someone will suggest they have a call. And they will speak and exchange stories again; they will discuss the reasons why it unravelled.

'Where did you go? After,' Gemz says. 'To Sammi's?'

'Not even.' She shakes her head. 'This is the thing. I was so embarrassed about the whole mess – Gemz, my credit score.'

Gemz's eyes widen.

'Yeah, payday loans. Credit-card debt. Everything.'

'Merce.'

'I really wanted to believe in it. When it collapsed, I went into denial. I would look at the numbers some days, like: this is not me.'

Gemz stops walking. All is quiet around them.

'So after that,' she continues, 'I moved back to Tottenham, my old place.'

'Tottenham.'

'Yeah, the same house where I was living before.'

'Ah, sweet. With the garden.'

They begin walking again, side by side. The earth is potholed, the mud studded with stones. The ground slopes up; the lake must be near.

'Only reason I got it was because the landlord knew me from before. I was walking dogs. The state of my credit score, no one else would rent to me.'

'Oh.'

'Dog-walking helped, though,' she says, and smiles.

Ahead is the slope that leads to the lake. The fragrance is stronger; the day tastes of algae and mud and silt.

She tells Gemz about Ekua. Of the chance to mentor others after this sit. A year complete, after this house, with enough experience to help others.

The lake appears at once: a pane of shifting sky. The water, taut, and settled within its restlessness. Circles ripple out from drops of rain. Here, by the water, she pushes her hood back.

40

It ends – and begins – here. With Gemz, by the water.

For finally, as promised, Gemz is back before the camera.

Nervous, though, as usual, she says, and laughs. 'God. I am not ready for this. Okay, but I am, though. We are doing this.'

Nervous, sure. But this is fine, this is it – closing the loop.

Mercy says, it's fine, it's chill. They can just sit.

Gemz bundles her coat up and slides her backpack off her shoulders. She drops it in the grass by her boots and settles down on the slope. The grass is thick, moments away from the water. In the shelter of the trees and the blossom, the earth looks reasonably dry. Gemz leans back on her hands and stretches her legs ahead of her.

'So when you sent the map,' she says, 'yesterday, I was looking at it and thinking, there's a lot of space, wherever this woman has taken herself.'

Mercy settles on the grass beside her. Sure enough, in the shelter of the boughs, the ground is only a little soft from the rain. It feels pliable, as if the earth is calling to be remoulded.

From behind, from the forest, there comes a bark.

Gemz flinches at the sound, and they both look back.

Another bark. A yap echoes, the sound ricocheting off all that is firm. And then there comes a voice – strained but certain. With this come more barks. Then another shout, another bark, again, a volley, a back-and-forth that echoes large before it fades. The sound grows dim until there is nothing, no trace of them, only the patter of drizzle on the foliage above.

'What was I saying?' Gemz says. Her face tilts up, eyes squinting in the light that filters through the green. She closes her eyes. 'But I mean. I kept thinking. I wanted to explain.'

Mercy shifts her own bag, the weight of the camera and lenses, onto her lap.

'Looking back,' Gemz continues, 'looking back now, sometimes I feel like. Well, I feel like I didn't properly try. Like I could have tried harder to explain, to be real with you. To tell you what was happening with me at the time. Instead of just leaving, the way I did. And I am sorry, because that was something I had promised myself I would not do.'

'Gemz.'

'No, really. I mean it. I want to say this. This is important to me. I promised myself. I told myself I would not hide from people I care about. That was a promise I made for Solomon, my cousin. Remember?'

'Of course,' she says. She tells Gemz she has been thinking about him lately. She has been thinking about a lot while alone here through these past weeks.

'He couldn't be real with us,' Gemz says. 'We didn't give him enough space.'

The day is still now; even the drizzle has stopped. The

only movement is on the surface of the lake ahead, as it laps the mud with its gilded edge.

'I'm tired. So I'm just going to say it,' Gemz says. She bows her head and her locs fall and curtain her face away. 'I'll just say it because I need to get it out, and this is not about you, or us. Nothing like that. At the time, I left because I had to – I needed to – be alone. I had to leave, to sit with this.' Gemz pulls her legs in, crosses them. 'I have this. So you know what I said, like with Solomon. With what I am pretty sure was OCD. And I'm sure that this runs in my family, in different ways. But. Yeah. I have something. I found out that I have a similar condition.'

It's complicated, she says. It is hard to describe how it feels. At times, she says, it feels like a kind of allergy, as though she cannot tolerate so many common sounds. She cannot, she has tried to, but it is too distressing to stay with them. Some noises trigger her, and even knowing that they could happen, just knowing it, she has to leave. It is not just about disliking some sounds, she says, it is not as simple as finding them irritating. It is visceral, she says. Literally, she has to avoid them. This is why, she says, she will never attempt to live in a shared house. Here, she laughs, a bitter sound. It is also why she has had to move so many times. Noise is very hard to escape, she says. Noise seeps into her studio, from the neighbours, and from the floor below, and in time it is too much, the place no longer feels like home. It happens in cycles, on and on, she has to move and start again. And the worst part of it, she says, was being unable to explain it up until now.

'I couldn't tell you about it at the time, Merce; I couldn't make sense of it in my own head at the time. And I think, in a way, part of me was also in denial then. I think that

Solomon may have felt like that at times, too. Like you know something is not right, something is off, you can feel it, but you can't see what exactly the problem is, and then around you there is no space to step away far enough for it to make sense. It's hard to just sit still with yourself and look at it.'

She has gone for years, she says, keeping this to herself.

'And it was my choice, in a way; I tried to keep it to myself. But. It made me angry, and it made me push people away. But I was hopeful, in a way, the whole time I kept this to myself. I think part of me hoped that it would sort itself out on its own.'

It's different now, she continues, now that she has found a name for it. With the name, it has become real. The name is a handle; she can pick it up now, hold it up. She can raise it to the light and look at it. She can see it. She can turn it over, now, and test its weight across her hands. Not a quirk. A mystery, sure, but real.

'I wanted space,' she says. 'When I first read about it. To work it out. To say to myself, fine, this is real. This is a thing. And it is. You can look it up. Actually, please do,' she says. 'I think. I can't explain it properly. They call it misophonia.'

'Gemz, I—'

Gemz waves. She is not finished. 'I went to Brighton for a while,' she says.

'Brighton.'

'Yeah, straight from your place. I went. Straight from Tottenham. No plans. Nothing.'

'Oh, you went back to your old place?'

'Kind of. I had to go. Merce, for real. I was thinking back, to the people I have already left because of this. I notice something, like a sound, something silly, something really trivial that they do without realising, then after that, it actually hurts to be near them. When I realised this was a thing, I just wanted to get away, to sit with it. So, in Brighton, I stayed with Ellie. On her boat. We smoked; Ellie is Ellie. She had not changed.' Gemz laughs. 'At all. We played a set. It was freshers' week, so we went back for old times' sake, and I was just seeing everything differently, the same but with this distance. That was when I called you, and I think, at that time, you had blocked me or something because—'

'I didn't block you. I must have changed my number by then,' Mercy says.

'You changed your number?'

'Yeah. They made us.'

'They?'

'So when I was in the church. We – they recommended it.'

'What?'

'Honestly, that was it. It was about switching off from the world.'

Gemz lifts her face. Her eyes are heavy.

'A clean break from your old self,' Mercy says. 'Don't let the past distract you. And Gemz, when you left, I mean – I wanted to start again. Because I was still not over what happened when I was at uni? That was my first relationship, I guess. And I really struggled to make sense of what happened. I was sure it would keep happening like this.'

'Like what?'

'Like I get close to something that feels real, and then it collapses. And the reason for the collapse is hard to see, out of my reach. I wanted to start again, when I joined the church. Most of us did. But go on. I interrupted you. Brighton.'

'Yeah,' Gemz says, 'Brighton. So I stayed with Ellie for a while. I used to get drunk and read about this condition on my laptop. It was the only way I could face it for a while. And from reading, like, with time, I realised, OK, so this is real. I realised I had to figure out how to live around this, so I read about other people who are doing it as well, and honestly, thank God for the internet. I read about other people's journeys, and I was thinking, uhh, Gemma, please, see it this way: you have already made it this far, and apparently quite a few others are living with this, too. So I said to myself, while I'm here, I have to try. I want to. For Solomon.

'So, Mercy, imagine, I started saving for a van. Yeah. This is the thing. I just need a place – I just need one place in this world that is mine. I don't understand why it has to be so difficult. Just a place in this world I can return to. Nothing fancy. So I said, look. I'll get a van and refit it. I will keep it moving; I can travel with it. I mean, why not? I'll do the tour – see New Orleans, for Solomon, and maybe I'll even go and travel Francophone Africa.

'You know, once I had that, once I decided to get the van, I felt a thousand times better. Not just about the future, but I felt better about where I was in the moment. Because now I am working towards a life that could be fun? I still don't know how far this thing will go. I've read that some people find that it gets worse, harder, with time. But I mean here, with the van, I feel like at least I have a way.'

'I want to say something,' Mercy says. 'But I'm just sitting here like, what?'

Gemz laughs. Her body shudders with it.

'I had,' Mercy says. 'I had a hundred theories I just kept turning over in my head. Because I know I was. Well. I mean, I know I could have done better – I could have given us more.'

'Merce,' Gemz says.

'Honestly. And that's what I kept thinking about, after you left.'

Gemz inclines her head, one eyebrow raised.

'I wish,' Mercy says, because now they are here, now they are on the edge, she may as well say. 'I know I could have pushed myself. Like how we never went to my parents' place. And my sister – she saw your photo and she asked about you a few times. But. Well. Stuff like that.'

Gemz is shaking her head. 'It's not about that,' she says. She sits forward and wipes drizzle from her brow. 'I mean. That stuff is, whatever. I get it. We were both still figuring it out. I left. Well, I left because of this.' She waves, gesturing towards herself. 'And when your friend messaged me the other day.'

'Ife?'

'Yes. I think so. Ife. Yeah. So when she reached out, I was thinking, when she said you were going to leave the UK soon, I was sitting in my studio thinking, like, with where I am right now, where I've reached, I can do this. I can be real. It is the least I can do. I had this feeling in Brighton, too. It was just like here, this clarity. And I realised, hey, there's space. More than enough space to at least try to be real.

'And I think that maybe this is part of the work. Creating space for each other. For ourselves, right? I know that for me' – she looks back, towards the lake. The clouds are shifting again, thickening to darker grey. 'For me,' she says, 'I know I need to keep moving. I do. If I stay still for long, I notice things.' She laughs. 'And not in a good way.'

41

It is after eight when they get back to the house. A glance then, for the first time, in hours, at the phone, now that, again, the signal is strong. Sure enough, new messages flood in. Some are in the x-kingdom group chat. And more messages are queued up waiting, from Ife.

In the kitchen, by the sink, Mercy swipes up through their chat. Ife has sent link after link to articles and videos, interspersed with blocks of text – questions. Ife has found the client's daughter on socials. They have mutual connections on LinkedIn, she says. With some digging she has found her Instagram and YouTube accounts as well.

Um. This girl has quite a following, she writes.

And:

> *Mercy. This is too much. Call me when you see this please.*

Mercy looks up, across the kitchen. Gemz is back with the empty glasses they left in the front room before the walk. She places them on the worktop and stretches. Both arms up.

42

Intentional, to choose this: to look away from these messages, to choose instead to remain here, in this house, with Gemz, in the present. It is not easy; these past weeks have been full of all but that. These have been weeks of memories and questions that reach beyond this house. These past days have been filled with thoughts, unbidden and otherwise, about elsewhere. But this space around them now is all they have.

And there is space. More with every hour. She will remember these last days in Meadowlight like this. Though it is ending, the truth of this sit, and of the houses that came before, with their numbers, all of which added up to this, the truth of these months is here, in these final days.

Gemz stays over. There is no choice: after the photos they are back at the house too late to catch the last train.

Time dissolves in the dining room, over pasta and more wine, and then Mercy shows her around the house.

Gemz says there is no way that there are cats still here in this house. The place is spotless. And it is too quiet.

'I reckon they slipped out,' she says. 'We should look properly in the morning. To double-check.'

If they have run, she says, they will not have gone far in this weather. They have time – they will look outside, when morning comes, and they can visit the neighbouring houses.

'I'm not going to lie, I don't even know where the nearest neighbour is,' Mercy says. They are back in the kitchen now, getting water before going to bed.

'Um. You haven't spoken to the neighbours?' Gemz looks appalled, comically stern, with her hair up in a bun. She is standing by the window against the darkness of the garden. 'Are you being serious?' she says.

'I know,' Mercy says. 'Let's just see in the morning.'

Over coffee, the following morning, she calls the driver from the first day. They will go from house to house, and ask. Someone must have seen them, with all the rain. Someone may have taken them in.

'That's the main reason I can think of that explains why they have stayed away,' Gemz says.

Mercy is trying not to think of the other reasons.

'What?' Gemz says.

'What?'

'You're making a face.'

'Just. I mean. That sounds too easy to be true.'

'Sometimes the problem is not as complicated as it feels inside your head,' Gemz says. 'You get stuck overthinking, Merce. This is so you.'

It is nice in the taxi, on the road after so long. The radio plays as they roll through the drizzle. The driver seems to be amused by the situation. He leans out of the window each time they stop, watches as they go to ring the doorbell.

'Any luck?' he asks, when they return and climb back in.

By the fourth house, Gemz is still optimistic. They have spoken to a pensioner, who has seen and heard nothing of any cats. They have spoken to a couple, who said they would keep an eye out in case, although sadly they too had not seen any cats recently. At the third house they spoke to students, at least five, who were dressed in waterproofs, lacing up their walking boots. The students said they may have heard something; they heard wailing in the night, which may have been cats, or foxes.

By house number four, they are almost five miles from Meadowlight.

'After this one,' Mercy says, 'I think we need to call it.'

'Yeah?' Gemz says.

'I need to call the client soon as well. I think it was supposed to be today that she was due to give her speech.'

'Today?'

'I think so. It will still be early now, but I reckon she will email or something soon.'

She will ask to see her cats. She will at least expect a photo by now.

And no doubt she will be nervous, superstitious before her speech.

'It's calm,' Gemz says. 'Don't overthink it. We'll see what happens and go from there.'

This next house is a bungalow, set behind a sprawling lawn. A middle-aged man opens the door, in a jumper over pale jeans. Close behind him is a woman, and another man. Another woman with a toddler in her arms. Two families, holidaying together, it seems.

Gemz says that they are looking for three missing cats.

'We have been asking in the area, because we suspect they have run away.'

The man looks back down the hallway. 'Missing cats,' he calls.

The woman comes nearer, towards the door. The toddler squirms in her arms.

'Hello,' the woman says. She is wearing an apron patterned with multicoloured handprints. 'Everything all right? Can we help you?'

Gemz explains it again: they are looking for three cats.

The woman lowers the infant to the floor. The child turns and toddles back down the hallway.

'Oh?' the woman says. 'Maybe we can help. The other day, we did actually find a . . .' She trails off. Instead she says, 'Oh actually. Do you have any photos? Or a description?'

43

Sankofa
Oyo
Ubuntu

Back at Meadowlight, with Gemz, she takes their photos in the hallway.

Mercy sends the images to the client that evening.

'I wanted you to see them before you give your speech,' she writes. 'Hope it goes well.'

Moments later, the client emails back. She says that she has changed her plans. Earlier that afternoon, she decided to pull out of the conference.

A second email follows, minutes later, a longer one. Mercy is at the top of the staircase when it comes in, and she sits on the last step to read the client's words.

The client writes that she made the decision to pull out of the conference after speaking with her daughter the other night. Her daughter, whom she has not spoken to in years, called her yesterday. She had questions. She called to ask who was staying at the house. Her daughter claimed to have seen photos of people staying there, on

Instagram. She claimed that someone had looked her up on LinkedIn, a lawyer, around her age, and unsettled, she had looked that lawyer up in return. She found her on Instagram, presumably one of Mercy's friends, the client writes, but her daughter was alarmed to see photos of Meadowlight on what appeared to be a stranger's page. She recognised the garden, in the background of those photos. She recognised the back wall outside the kitchen. The client writes that she and her daughter had a long back-and-forth on the call. It was something. We rarely speak, she said; we are quite different, as people. She says she was surprised to hear how much her daughter had grown, how she seemed to have settled into herself since they'd last spoken. They had a wonderful conversation in the end, she said. And yes, it meant that she did not have time to rehearse her speech as she had planned, so she decided to pull out of the conference. She has felt no excitement about it lately, she writes. Speaking to her daughter made this clearer, helped her to admit it. The amount of time she has spent worrying, trying to perfect the speech. It has brought her more stress and worry than anything else. And to this day, she is still not content with it. Perhaps it is a sign, she writes, that the timing is not quite right, and maybe, for now, that is fine. This trip has turned out to be about something more than the speech itself. She will always treasure this break as her first time away from the house in years.

A third email follows, minutes after this. Mercy is in the study now, at the desk, about to start her laptop up. She props her phone against the screen and reads the client's words.

The client writes that she has been thinking about the

distance between herself and her daughter. How until they spoke recently, she had always thought of it as settled, fixed. She writes that her daughter built a following on social media. Unfortunately, she built that following largely through carrying out pranks, through years of misbehaving in public and filming it. Her videos have become increasingly disturbing over the years. The client says she felt helpless, watching her daughter spiral away. At times she wondered what might have happened if she had never let her use a computer. She could do nothing to draw her back. Any attempts to reason with her only pushed her further away. When they spoke yesterday, she says, it was the first time they discussed it properly, with distance, and with more space to look back and reflect. She can see it now, she says, her daughter is moving on now, still growing.

Gemz stays again, for another night. And then another, and the following day. She is here, too, the afternoon Mercy's mother calls.

They are in the study when the call comes. Rain has chased them back inside after a hike. Mercy is at the desk planning tutorials for the week. Gemz is on the carpet with her laptop and headphones, layering silences.

Then it comes: a call flashes on the phone under the desk.

There and then not. A missed call, as before. When she looks closely, it is Mother. This time her profile photo is a vaguely familiar face. A man with white hair, light reflecting off square glasses; a family friend who recently passed away. The photo fills the screen and then disappears.

Not a missed call, then, as she had thought; this is a call that stopped before it could begin. The call is a flashing signal, a hand extending – dissolving.

'Gemz,' she says. And when Gemz doesn't appear to hear, she waves.

'What's up?'

'Nothing.' She props the phone on the desk against the monitor. 'Just need to call my mum.'

Gemz slides her headphones back, and watches, one eyebrow up.

Mercy puts the phone on speaker. She turns the volume up.

A normal conversation. Overdue, maybe. Sure.

A relief, in some way, for here, between them, despite all these months, despite the distance, nothing has changed. Mother says, as before, her room is still there in the flat. The room is there, and always will be, if she ever needs a place. There is no need to live in strangers' houses like that, she says.

It has been too long since they last spoke, she continues. She says she heard from Ife's mother that the girls – her friends from school – had got together for a day out, that the four of them had a beautiful day out of London. She says that she saw a photo of them together, in a garden, young women now. It's wonderful, she says. The Lord is good.

'That is all I'm asking for, Mercy,' she says. 'Make time for others in this life, please, and no matter what happens, you have to remember where you came from. We have all been praying for you. We have. Whenever you're doing well, you should know it is because we are still praying for you. No one is perfect, my baby, just do your best. Iron sharpens iron. You cannot do your best alone.'

Across the room, Gemz waves. There is a question in her gaze.

'I don't understand you,' Mother says. 'Well. Anyway, that is not the point. It's not for us to understand. God is the author and finisher of your life. You know the path that is righteous; as for me, I know that I've done my part. Anyway, I didn't mean to call you. I will leave you to enjoy the rest of your day now. And please, send the photos. I shouldn't have to get them from Ife's mum, o.'

44

On the last day, before leaving, here, too, it helps to make a list.

To do:

One final sweep
Check the house – from room to room
Reset the furniture to how it was on the first day
And: call Ekua.

None of these sits would have happened without her help.

She dials her number in the hallway, by the door. And it rings. And rings. And rings.

And then a text: hey. can't speak now – on a call (about the house!)

Outside, the day is mild; the sky is open, powder blue.

The road is clear.

Here is the cab from the first day, pulling up now with its light.

Acknowledgements

Thank you to my agent, Juliet Mushens, and editor, Francesca Main, for the advice, patience and encouragement. I am grateful to the wider team at Phoenix Books for their work and support throughout. Special thanks to my copy-editor, Eleanor, for her insight and sensitivity.

My love and gratitude to my friends, who were also my first co-dreamers, including Kevine, my almost-sister; I'm doing it and I miss you still. To Rosie, for imagining with me, and for the sensitivity and kindness throughout our girlhood. To Eva, for What Happens Next, and the stories we shared. To Erene, for the laughter, dancing, music, and the tea that night in Clapham. For Pride, and so many wonderful memories across London and beyond through our twenties. To Manolis, for the voice notes and encouragement while I grappled with this novel. To Peggy, for our conversations, for the yellow flower, for dancing with me in Norwich and being so polite with the dead. To G, for our lockdown chats, and the provocations and lessons. To D and the kickboxing gang, who kept me fighting and embodied. S, for your company, and for that beautiful afternoon we climbed a tree. To Orlaine and Marie-Claire, for your wisdom and encouragement. To Troy, Laia and Deshawn, for the dancing, for listening. To the rest of the music gang – David, Lucas, Tom it's been so fun and restorative playing together post-pandemic. To Jefferson, for your friendship, philosophising, coffee and wine. For a beautiful time in Kuala Lumpur, where this story began again.

I'm forever thankful to my family: to my brother, for insisting that I read, for the music, and for picking the bass up so quickly. To my dad, the Rhymer, for teaching me how to find x, break words down and finish hard. For all the lifts. To my mum, for letting me have the living room to dance with the surround sound system some nights, for giving me space. To my sister, for teaching me to journal and gifting me *The Color Purple*, my first glimpse. For late night storytelling and organising the midnight feasts. To Auntie Adjoa, for keeping it real, and yet so positive and full of care. To my cousins, for showing up and for the memories.

About the author

Sussie Anie is a British-Ghanaian writer, born in London in 1994. Her writing has been published in *Lolwe*, and was shortlisted for the 2020 White Review Short Story Prize. She has an MA in Creative Writing from the University of East Anglia, where she was the recipient of the Kowitz Scholarship. Her first novel, *To Fill a Yellow House*, won the Somerset Maugham Award.

RAISING READERS

Books Build Bright Futures

Dear Reader,

We'd love your attention for one more page to tell you about the crisis in children's reading, and what we can all do.

Studies have shown that reading for fun is the **single biggest predictor of a child's future life chances** – more than family circumstance, parents' educational background or income. It improves academic results, mental health, wealth, communication skills, ambition and happiness.[1]

The number of children reading for fun is in rapid decline. Young people have a lot of competition for their time. In 2024, 1 in 10 children and young people in the UK aged 5 to 18 did not own a single book at home.[2]

Hachette works extensively with schools, libraries and literacy charities, but here are some ways we can all raise more readers:

- Reading to children for just 10 minutes a day makes a difference
- Don't give up if children aren't regular readers – there will be books for them!
- Visit bookshops and libraries to get recommendations
- Encourage them to listen to audiobooks
- Support school libraries
- Give books as gifts

There's a lot more information about how to encourage children to read on our website: **www.RaisingReaders.co.uk**

Thank you for reading.

hachette UK

---

[1] OECD, '21st-Century Readers: Developing Literacy Skills in a Digital World', 2021, https://www.oecd.org/en/publications/21st-century-readers_a83d84cb-en.html

[2] National Literacy Trust, 'Book Ownership in 2024', November 2024, https://literacytrust.org.uk/research-services/research-reports/book-ownership-in-2024